Roswell
Boneyard

Portals of Yahweh
Book 1

Joe Greer

Roswell Boneyard

Published by Distributed Sensing Solutions

First edition: June 2020

Cover Design by: SelfPubBookCovers.com/ RLSather

To my mother Drucilla, she always knew I would build the spaceships I drew as a boy.

Contents

Prologue

1943

The telephone rang in an enormous old mansion in the center of Sao Paulo. A mansion built in 1868 by cotton farmers from the defeated confederacy brought to Brazil to develop plantations. It was haunted with the psychic reek of self-important people made rich by the sweat and pain of others.

The maid answered, "de Mello residency how may I help you?"

"Cameron de Mello please, this is an old business associate, Quarnar." The voice sounded very funny as if from a radio broadcast.

"One moment"

When Cameron answered he was hyperventilating. "You said twenty years, it's been thirty. My treatment is past due." Cameron was in bad shape. Jaundiced, his skin starting to sag. Deep dark circles ringed his sunken eyes.

"I was busy, but I am here now above your planet and I have your elixir," Quarnar responded testily.

"You are looking for more of the same?"

"Yes"

"It is a good time for buyers. Meet me at my country residence in one revolution."

The next day Cameron de Mello walked into a small wood behind his country house carrying a small valise. This was their traditional meeting point. An insect nearly as tall as himself that looked like a praying mantis but with thicker shoulders and a big head moved slowly toward him carrying a device in its claw.

"I came alone Quarnar, you can point that away from me."

"This is a violent planet. One must be careful. Tell me the situation for buying." Quarnar's translator said after some chittering. Insects are not much for small talk.

"You must take me to the European continent. A very big war is happening, and the leaders are quite ruthless with the population."

"Perfect, I require twenty thousand, of which three fourths should be strong males."

"You will need to take away more and cull them to get your goal."

"Agreed" Quarnar made the Galactic circling motion which signified a closed agreement. No need to point out that the lowest valued would make protein paste for the rest. Humans had a strange aversion to eating their own. It was going to be a long journey and feeding was too major of an expense. Protein is scarce and expensive in the wider Galaxy. "Your one thousand kilos of gold will be left in the usual building. Here is your medicine."

Cameron took the applicator and immediately injected himself. He had brought food in the valise to take advantage of the nanites as quickly as possible. Too many years had passed, and he could feel his body had deteriorated farther than it should. "Alright, go to your ship and I will bring my car to load on board."

The two days later, Cameron got out of a Duesenberg Phaeton and walked up to the front gate of a concentration camp in Poland. It had been very easy to find several from orbit. This one had the best approaches for their venture.

"I need to talk to your Commandant please" he told the guard in broken German. "My group wants to hire the labor of your residents."

"Wait here."

A few minutes later another guard led him into the main office. The secretary looked at him very skeptically. She said "Commandant Linmacher will see you. Through that hall, do not deviate."

"Good morning sir."

"Good morning. What brings you to our lovely facility?" Linmacher replied.

"I am interested in buying the services of twenty thousand of your residents on a permanent basis."

The secretary came in just then with a coffee service. They waited for her to serve and leave.

"That is a very big number Mr....?"

"de Mello of Brasil. And yes, it is. I need three fourths to be strong males."

"For your coffee plantation? I must let you know right now these things will not be released for any price." The Commandant said, "I would be shot."

"I understand but they would not be left alive here on Earth. This would be a final solution for your problem."

"That is the most ridiculous statement I have ever heard. For wasting my time maybe, you should waste some of yours here as our guest."

"The car I arrived in has fifty kilos of gold. It is yours if you let me prove my ability to do what I say. There is another two hundred and fifty for the purchase." De Mello replied hastily.

There was a long pause as he reappraised the situation. "Well let's go look," the gleam of greed shone in Linmacher's eyes.

They walked back through the gate and Cameron opened the trunk of the Duesenberg. He then opened a wooden ammunition box to reveal the five bars. Linmacher pulled a pen knife out and made several scratches to check it was not just a veneer. He called two guards over and instructed them to carry the box into his office.

"Now show me." he challenged.

"Please place this in your ear. That way I can speak my native Portuguese and you can understand much better."

Linmacher reluctantly did as requested. He was after all newly rich by this man. The technology amazed him, but de Mello told him to wait for explanations. De Mello drove ten miles to the south on a dirt road until he came to a large lake by the railway being feed by a small river.

He lifted a small radio and said, "We are ready for the demonstration Quarnar."

A few moments later a huge spaceship lifted out of the water and hovered at fifty meters for two minutes. It then slowly sank back into the water. Linmacher's mouth was still hanging open as the craft disappeared.

"Would you like to go aboard?"

Linmacher just nodded. Soon a tube snaked up and out of the water like a tentacle. The end irised open.

"It is not of this world?"

"No, but it has been here many times for trade. Just imagine what the Indians of North America thought when they saw the first European ships. This is why I said the labor will not be left on Earth alive," de Mello explained. "I will not introduce you to the owner of this craft. He is shy and afraid of human's fear reaction to insectoids."

"Insectoid?"

"Yes, my partner is a giant praying mantis. Doesn't matter. You will see that it is nicely set up to control large numbers of livestock." de Mello gave a brief tour. "This cage contains the humans who will attend to the others in route."

They looked down on about one hundred miserable looking men. Physically strong but obviously broken in spirit.

"The trip back takes about eight weeks I understand." Cameron responded to a few more questions, none of which were the least bit relevant then said, "Let us go back and discuss the details of delivery."

Linmacher nodded suddenly pensive. "I want the car too."

"Yes," de Mello responded with some hesitation, "that is possible."

Delivery was as easy as stopping trains and herding the contents into the water tunnel. 'New way to implement the final solution,' was all the explanation necessary to the train personnel. All was progressing nicely and then Linmacher was caught driving around in his Duesenberg by the Gestapo. Driving spoils of war in itself was not forbidden, but sporting about the buxom girl with high cheekbones certainly was. She was the Gestapo commander's favorite prostitute. Linmacher's new wealth led from one question to another since the girl was notoriously expensive. Then Linmacher was getting personal attention in the Gestapo basement. The next train did not stop. Panzers started lining up on the lake shore and Quarnar decided it was time to shop elsewhere.

"We are still short five thousand men. My order was specific on the number of strong men. On the plus side, children are a bonus." Quarnar buzzed his irritation. "I need to leave within two weeks to fulfill my commitment."

"Let's go see what we can get from the Russians, they have prison camps too."

"Men?"

"Both but maybe we can specify."

With a final irritated buzz of his vestigial wings. They moved east.

The Russian gulags had no railway. They were mainly lumber and dam construction camps in the forest.

"If I have to make deals to get just two or three hundred per camp, it will take too long. Besides if just one of the commandants is a fanatic or fear we are NKVD secret police, they would kill me. Time for a change in our method of operation."

"What do you propose?"

"We do it the old fashion way. Extreme violence. Your ship passes low overhead to get their attention. We call out with loudspeakers for all to move to the center of the camp. The guards will of course go to the towers and along the barbed wire. We burn the guards down with the plasma cannon. Land and call out to prisoners to march inside because they are being liberated on Stalin's order."

"We will lose the guards." Quarnar pointed out.

"Twenty or thirty maybe but it will be much faster. We keep it simple. After we scoop up as many as possible, we burn the rest of the camp. The winter will take care of survivors. The few left will not be believed." de Mello went on, "three camps per day and with luck only three days until you are full."

"If we do not see good results on the first day what would be the next idea?"

"Italy. Set up at the end of a railway tunnel in front of a troop train. Disable the locomotive and drive the passengers forward with gas. These will be armed soldiers so more care will be needed to control them inside."

"Soldiers make strong slaves, but they would make a mess until we knocked them out. Let's try the Russian gulags first."

It turned out the gulags were bigger and the inmates more docile than expected. They filled the rest of the quota in two days.

Cameron de Mello arrived back at his coffee plantation a happy man. He was much richer and recently reinvigorated with nanites, he looked ten years younger. The peon who saddled his horse asked what he wanted to inspect first.

"Take me out to the coffee harvest first, then by the slave quarters. I want to pick a strong woman for tonight." Cameron replied. Slavery had been outlawed in 1888 but not everyone in Brazil believed in that inconvenient law.

Roswell Boneyard

∞

The Artemis Accords signed in Singapore, July 2020; Provides for corporate ownership of assets on the moon, and for safety zones around moon bases to prevent interference. Signatories were Canada, Japan, USA, UK, India, and other like-minded countries. China denounced the accords and declared ownership of the moon in its entirety because of historical cultural importance to the Han people.

China using the cover of the war in the South China Sea decided to make good use of their commando teams. Because the cyber hacking team in Shanghai had been hit early in the war and were unable to function, China sent special forces in PLA uniforms to the NewOrigins space facilities at Port Aransas, Texas. It was quickly taken over and pillaged of all technology at hand. The troops stayed long enough to steal the hard drives for the entire NewOrigins booster program before retreating to Mexico. Over two hundred technicians, engineers and scientists were murdered behind the assembly building. This was exactly what China needed to suddenly become a true rival of the USA in space. In the next month, China was utterly defeated in the South China Sea effectively losing its entire navy. The threat to Taiwan was greatly diminished. It was imperative the Chinese Communist Party, CCP, find a new excuse to cling to power. Space was the only prestige arena available, so they started building and launching using stolen technology with all the energy they had previously placed in their military buildup. The moon had become the new South China Sea. No one could control it effectively without a strong presence. China began a military buildup on their lunar base to coincide with a newly formulated political propaganda declaring the moon was

China's by historical right. Chinese early astronomical observations in the BC era proved they were the first to claim it.

The US government, eager to recover from the economic devastation caused by the disruption of USA-China trade and the global Covid pandemic, slashed spending in every area. The contracts given to the space industries' private sector were zeroed out. The new Space Force struggled with keeping the lunar base manned as well as continue normal operations of satellites. Politicians had turned a blind eye to China's new campaign reasoning the CCP would drop the nonsense when it regained a strangle hold on the populous. They could not have been more wrong.

Hard Beginnings

This was going to be the most difficult day of h
Oliver was trying to get his younger brother out of
have a last talk with their dying mother.

"Jed, come out and have some Lucky Charms. We have to go soon." Oliver said to his brother curled up under the covers. "Hiding in bed changes nothing. This will be the last time we can talk to her. She has been off the pain medication so she could talk to us today. She is in a lot of pain, let's not keep her waiting."

"Why can't she have pain medication? I don't want her to go away like dad."

"When she is on the meds she can't think. It isn't her choice to die now. She fought it hard as she could. You know eventually, we all die anyway. Her time just came earlier than it should." Oliver explained again.

Jed started shaking and curled up even tighter. Oliver opened the Zoloft bottle and cut one of the pills in half.

"I know you don't like these, but this is the last time. No more after today, promise. Do it for her because she loves you and wants to see you one last time."

Jed sat up with these words and took the pill. He was still shaking but trying to take back control of his body. After ten minutes, he crawled out of bed and pulled on his jeans and a T-shirt. Bad day for everyone. It was a short drive to the hospital in his mother's Civic. Roswell is a small town. They walked past the nurse's station like so many times before but this time the nurses had no greeting and avoided their eyes. Mom was

14

ghtly propped up in bed. She opened her eyes as they walked in. The sound of a son's footsteps is hardwired into a mother's brain.

Oliver and Jed sat beside their mother's hospital bed. It took a few minutes before she found the strength to speak. "I have arranged with the judge to declare you competent as an adult Oliver. Take care of your brother at home. Since the house is paid off, the settlement money should see you through high school and four years of university. Jed, you do what your brother tells you. Stay together no matter what."

"Yes mother, Jed and I will be OK," Oliver responded.

"Come, both of you give me a hug. Not too tight, I love you both so much" she whispered with tears in her eyes.

Oliver and Jed on her two sides enveloped her and kissed her cheeks.

"Please call the nurse and tell her I will accept pain management again," Mildred said as her light green eyes glazed over with the pain. Terminal cancer had reduced this hard-working widow to a ghost of a person in six months. She had endured three days without pain meds so she could have this last conversation with her boys. Oliver, her eldest, overly serious for his age and Jed so incredibly brilliant but unable to cope with people. If they stayed together, they would make it. She was sure.

The nurse came in and turned on the morphine drip. Mildred, unable to talk anyway, laid there giving out small grunts from the pain. Oliver left the room with his eyes streaming. Jed following along in a trance. That was the last time they saw their mother alive.

∞

A week later, Oliver sat across from Mr. Howe, the family lawyer, who pushed a small stack of paper in front of Oliver.

"Mr. Eversole, the top document is your Emancipation. It was a good thing Judge Dewey knew your mother personally otherwise child protective service would have you and your brother in a foster home and probably cheated you out of your house. But here is the deed to the property on Elm Street in both your names, the title to the Honda Civic and transfers of bank accounts. You have all the tools to make this work if you don't start acting out like a teenager. Really this is too bad. A young person should not have to shoulder these responsibilities."

"Thank you, Mr. Howe, I promised my mother I would take care of Jed and that is exactly what I will do. There will be time enough for fun later."

Oliver left the lawyer's office with a zip lock folder of papers. He had turned 17 three weeks ago. At least he had all summer before his senior year in high school to work things out.

∞

Oliver did not feel the least bit guilty. The Honda was a car for a middle age lady not him. The money from the Honda had been enough to buy a 2000 SS Camaro T-top and a relatively new Yamaha 400 motorcycle. The Camaro was in rough shape but he, with the complete mechanic's shop in the garage that was his father's pride, would restore it. He was determined and

16

knew he had the knack with machinery. The first day of class he would not arrive in a Civic but in a man's car.

"Give me half a pump on the hoist," Oliver asked.

Jed complied and the last bolt on the motor mount came free. They pushed the shop hoist with the motor dangling over to the work bench and set it into a cradle of wood blocks. After an hour of pulling parts off the block, Oliver took a step back wiping his hands.

"The block is in better shape than I hoped but the cam shaft and pistons will tell the real story. Let's get cleaned up and go buy something to eat. What do feel like Jed?"

"Mrs. Ortiz and the park."

"A Mexican picnic it is then. You ok with the motorbike?"

"Well, I don't want to push the Camaro."

Oliver laughed and said, "Right you are. Let's go as we are. Mrs. Ortiz won't mind greasy clothes if we get takeout."

Sitting on the park bench building a taco, Oliver was watching his brother. He seemed the same as always.

"Jed, riding the motorbike doesn't upset you?"

"In the Honda, I felt safe." Jed said and paused a few moments before continuing, "Mom is gone. It is not the same, but I feel ok riding behind you, and we will get the Camaro running pretty soon. Hopefully before winter." The last he said with a crooked smile and started building his next taco.

∞

"Mrs. Mackie, I am Jed's brother and legal guardian. Can we talk a little?"

"Yes Oliver, I am aware of the new situation. I am sorry about your mother."

Jed entered the gifted students' classroom and went to his desk turned toward the wall in the corner.

"I just wanted to let you know, I am taking care of Jed and if there are any problems call me. The principal already knows. Since I will be looking over his schoolwork, what are the things I need to do?"

"The work itself is probably beyond you already. Your brother is truly exceptional. His anxiety is controllable if you are careful. He doesn't like to participate but he enjoys being on the edge watching others. You know some of this I am sure but having responsibility for it is different. Try to maintain him in familiar settings but do not go to excess. Over the years his anxiety should get milder." Audrey Mackie said then added, "He has a wry sense of humor. I enjoy that about him."

"You are right, knowing and being responsible are two different things," Oliver said. "Bell is going to ring soon. Thanks Mrs. Mackie."

Lunch time was the usual loud chaos. Oliver's friend Carl waved him over. Betty and Midge were yakking on about some new Rom-Com at the cinema. Carl was trying to stay close enough to Betty to see the swell of her breasts. Some things never change.

"I heard you bought some piece of shit Camaro," Carl said.

"It may be a piece of shit now, but it won't be after I restore it."
Oliver responded.

"Dude, you really going to do that by yourself?"

"My dad left me a complete mechanic shop and I learn by
doing."

"More power to you then. I wouldn't have the patience.
Football practice leaves me drained anyway. And Betty drains
the rest."

"Dream on big boy." Betty retorted.

"I'll ride in it with you. After you paint it. Hey, maybe you could
put some cool go-fast stripes on." Midge piped up.

"You can pick the color Midge," Oliver said which made Midge
blush with pleasure.

"Metallic silver strips on red." She said without hesitation.

"Beautiful," Oliver said looking into her honey brown eyes.

And then the bell rang. Back to class.

∞

A month later, Oliver offered to take Midge home after school
in the restored Camaro with metallic silver stripes. Jed sat down
on the floorboards of the back seat. He didn't want to see the
new person. Instead of taking Midge home, they cruised the
Main Street for an hour letting the whole town see Midge in the
hot rod with the hot boy. Oliver knew girls valued such things
and he didn't mind since Midge rubbed him the whole time. She
didn't even seem to realize she was doing it. He missed his

mom, but life goes on. The next week after cruising, he took her to his house and popped her cherry along with his.

The months crept by schoolwork and cruising with Midge made life bearable. Keeping the bills paid on time was not difficult after the first time the power was turned off. Responsibility, Oliver found out was more a matter of setting up the calendar on his smart phone. No big deal if you stay ahead of it.

Midge learned about insisting on going to parties after Oliver laid out the bare facts one afternoon while they were sitting at the Sonic with greasy burgers. Jed was sitting on the floorboard in back, as per his habit, doing calculus homework. Midge started in about the big Christmas party her friend was having while the parents were on a ski trip.

"If Jed is smart enough to do calculus why can't he stay home alone? We never go anywhere alone. I want to show you off." She whined.

"Smart has nothing to do with it. He is ten years old and for all the reasons you already know, doesn't cope with outsiders. Babysitters just don't work."

"Don't I take care of you in that special way? Maybe we shouldn't do it so much."

"Suit yourself but Jed and I are the team, end of story. We. Stay. Together. If you want to play on our team, that is the rule." Oliver answered emphatically. Midge finished her burger, got out of the car and called an Uber.

Betty showed up at Oliver's house on Christmas afternoon with a giant box of leftover dinner. Carl had kicked her to the curb when she wouldn't 'take care' of some of his football buddies.

Betty 'took care' of Oliver until he moved to Socorro for school and her, to Stanford University. Jed liked her. She was smart.

∞

Barbara "Babs" Whiting and her sister-wife Terry Whiting were driving a herd of one hundred yearlings down from the high pastures in the Sacramento mountains of New Mexico. They had reached the core area of the ranch and were in the corridor between pastures. They could see flashing lights near their house. Lights were also flashing near the houses of other families of the True Mormon Branch church. Barbara was leading the front of the herd and stopped just past the gate she had opened into the holding paddock when the lead steers began to balk. Looking behind her, she saw two Sherriff's Deputies walking toward her.

"What is wrong with you?" Babs shouted, "get on the other side of the fence and make yourself small or this herd is going to trample the life out of you."

The deputies not being totally country ignorant did as directed, the cattle settled down and turned on into the paddock. As Terry brought up the rear and closed the gate the deputies walked toward them again.

"Babs are there provisions up at High Camp?" Terry asked.

"Yes, I took some up in a cart last week," Babs said.

One of the deputies grabbed the reins of Babs horse and the other made a grab at Terry's, but her horse shied.

"Are you Barbara Whiting, married to Jonah Whiting?"

"Yes, but people call me Babs. This is my sister-wife, Terry."

"When did you marry Jonah?" the male deputy asked.

"About four years ago, why?"

"How old are you?"

"Almost seventeen. What is this about?"

"How old is your husband Jonah?"

"He is fifty-seven," Babs answered confused by the line of questioning.

"I am sorry Babs. Hopefully, I will see you again someday," Terry said as she wheeled her horse. She took off at a fast canter.

One of the deputies got on the radio. "We got a runner. Headed west on horseback."

"Please come down off your horse child. We will walk back to the stables. Along the way, I will explain. My guess is you have never been away from your community," the woman deputy said.

"I get to go to Artesia a couple of times a year to help with shopping," Babs argued.

"You have been the victim of child sexual abuse," she replied.

Babs responded vehemently, "No, I most certainly have not. My oldest sister-wife always stayed in the room when I was being with Jonah. That way he would not be too forceful, me being young and all. But he never hurt me."

The two deputies looked at each other with a sad expression.

∞

Roswell Boneyard

The next year of Babs life was both confusing and brutal. She was taken in front of a judge still crusty from sweat and trail dust. He declared she must stay with a foster family until eighteen or starting university. The state would guarantee up to four years of post-secondary school. Of course, Babs did not understand anything going on around her.

Babs foster family lived in Jal, NM. The so-called town was a collection of rusted, derelict oil field equipment, clapboard houses, one grocery store and one church. The Body of Christ Holiness Union. Her foster family headed by Alvin and Patty Olson were avid followers of the local preacher.

Her Mormon church had been closed to the outside world, but they were loving and supportive to those that stayed. That is not counting all the sons who were expelled to fend for themselves at eighteen. All the daughters stayed, of course. Everyone worked and everyone ate. Homeschooling was mandated by the church and consisted of the three Rs and two Bs. Reading, Riting, Rithmatic, Bible and the Book of Mormon.

The church in Jal was another matter entirely. The Olson family gave most of their money to the church, so there was little left over for the many foster children to eat. Keeping foster children was the family's livelihood. The fostered were being raised as true believers which is all that mattered. To keep them on the straight and narrow, the slightest infraction was punished by a caning and days locked in the basement. While in reflection time, a single bowl of soup beans and pone of corn bread per day were given to sustain the physical body. No more was considered needed.

No one spoke of going to school. To the authorities, the fosters were being homeschooled. Homeschooling in the Olson family consisted of a stack of old grammar, physics, math and American history books stacked in a corner. Reading was a group exercise in the Bible. Unnoticed to most, there was a university level book on Fortran programming. Babs memorized the only logical thing in her new environment. To keep herself sane while in the basement, she wrote lines of code in her mind to solve the high school physics exercises. This was her pious reflection. The focus needed to do this formed her mind in a way that would later transform her life and that of the whole world.

Alvin and his three eldest sons were complete hypocrites. They would come down the stairs, thumping in their boots, to talk about her soul while she was in reflection time. Babs's genetic makeup was different from most people, which was manifest by having one brown eye and one blue. Generations of selective breeding by her ancestors had created a truly sensuous woman with full lips and a busty, voluptuous figure. The Olsen men were captivated, indeed even obsessed, by her physical presence. Unfortunately, the different eye colors transformed her, in their mind, to a demon. Invariably, they ended up forcing themselves on her, always promising that the caning would go easier next time. They became slaves to their lust.

By the end of her time in Jal, each day saw the four of them coming down to take her, then cane her, because she was forcing them into sin. Every day, one after the other. The last two months, she never saw the light of day. If another year were to pass, it was obvious they would have ended up killing her. As it was, they left her back crisscrossed with scars.

Two weeks before she would be taken to the university by the state, Alvin hung himself. Babs had convinced him in the week before that she was in fact an angel, not a demon. Her encyclopedic knowledge of the Bible proved it. It was something she had hidden over the year because so many of her beliefs were interlaced with the Book of Mormon. Mormons and Evangelicals had been feuding since the time of Joseph Smith. Patty buried his ashes in a Folgers coffee can next to a junk 1983 Chevrolet pickup truck. Patty shed no tears.

∞

The couple with their teenage son were sitting in a boat fishing. They were not catching anything even though they were in the Pantanal, Brazil's huge western swamp and premier fishing location. Each year the flat terrain was flooded for a few months bringing in nutrients like the Florida Everglades. Fish grew numerous but when the water receded to the many lagoons and lakes, they became overcrowded and hungry. Maybe the fish sensed the sour mood.

"I feel really sad you are getting a divorce."

"Marco, your mother and I have not lived together for a year now. We stayed together longer so you would have stable teenage years. Now that you will be going to university in America, we knew it was the right time." Hector said.

Marli added, "This ranch is yours now. It has been in my family for one hundred years so you must always come back every year. You must never neglect our family patrimony. Your father and I can be civil together, this not a problem, so every year we can go fishing like this as a family."

"Better than nothing, I guess. Maybe if we go fishing every year you two can be friends again and we can do more together." Marco replied bitterly. "I don't feel like fishing anymore. Can we just go back?"

"Yes let's. We had the talk, and no one shouted. That's enough to be grateful for." Hector said as he reached for the outboard motor's pull rope. Half an hour later they reached the dock on the creek running through the family ranch. Marco got in the back of his father's pickup to ride back to the main house. At least the DaSilvas would have some beef ribs on the fire slow roasting. Sad as he was the thought of the ribs made him start salivating. He was tall and skinny now, but with an appetite destined for a very big man.

Two weeks later Marco was driving down the Rio Grande Valley toward his new school in Socorro NM. Good thing the Americans liked pickup trucks. Helped him feel more at home. The air of New Mexico is super clear, and the stark landscape could be seen in detail from a long distance. There was no humidity to blur the distant mountains. The scope of the land was so large it seemed the car crept along in slow motion. In the valley bottom, cottonwood trees traced a narrow green line on the banks of the Rio Grande river otherwise only low scrub held onto the rock and sand.

"Well Toto," Marco said to his imaginary dog, "not much here. It certainly is not Sao Paulo. New life in a new land. New Mexico, Land of Enchantment. Ooof, whose idea was this?"

School Days

Babs had been in rude good health before being sent to Jal. She had arrived at the beginning of her foster care with D cup breasts, flat belly and a bubbled butt pinned in tight. Her auburn hair with sun bleached streaks, many a Hollywood actress would have given up silicon for. Youth and vibrancy gave her a beauty cosmetic companies would deny was real. Her dual eye color caught everyone's attention. After a year, most of which had been spent underground, she was skin and bones. Her hair looked like straw. She had turned into a scarecrow. Finally, August arrived, and the child protective service agent drove her to start university in Socorro, NM. The same agent who delivered her into the hands of the Olsons. No mention was made of Babs change in health.

Her new roommate Mosi, a Navajo girl, took pity and showed Babs around campus. They ended up at the cafeteria. The pass cards got them in with a beep and Babs saw the hot food steam tables, salads, desserts and drink machines. It was full of normal young people having dinner. Tears started running down her cheeks and she had to go sit against the wall. The nightmare was over.

∞

Marco was sitting in the back of the lecture hall waiting for the first class of Advanced Quantum Mechanics to begin. This was the start of his senior year and he was feeling very content living in America. In the back of his mind, he was formulating a plan to stay. Two boys, one an obvious freshman and a kid about ten came up and asked if they could sit down.

"Hi, my name is Oliver, and this is my brother Jed. I have a strange favor to ask."

"You do seem out of place, strange would be expected," Marco replied.

"Jed is far ahead of me in physics. Quantum mechanics intrigues him, so I promised he could sit in on this class."

Marco was perplexed.

"The thing is, he has extreme anxiety since becoming an orphan and doesn't cope well when out of the familiar. Could he simply sit next to you during the semester? He really is no bother and simply sitting next to the same person each day reduces his stress. That way he can concentrate on the material."

"Yeah, not a problem, but you do realize this is a graduate level course on quantum mechanics?"

"I am aware. By the way, he may occasionally write a question for you to ask the professor. Don't worry though, they will be good questions," Oliver said.

"Okay"

Just then, the professor stepped up to the lectern and said, looking pointedly at Oliver and Jed, "I am Dr. Meriwether Lee, and this is Advanced Quantum Mechanics, PHY507. If you are not in the right class, you know what to do."

Oliver got up patted his brother on the shoulder and left. Dr. Lee just raised an eyebrow.

∞

Roswell Boneyard

A couple of weeks after the semester had started, Oliver and Jed were looking for a table to sit in the food court of the Student Union. Jed nudged Oliver in the side and pointed with his chin at a table with just one girl by herself. She was skinny and had hair that looked like it was a Halloween fright wig.

"Mind if we sit with you? Tables are kind of full today." Oliver asked.

"Help yourself," Babs responded. "Not many people want to sit with me. They think I have a disease or something."

"Doesn't look like anything a lot of good meals would not cure."

"Exactly," Babs said enthusiastically. "I am Babs Whiting."

"Oliver Eversole and this is my brother Jed."

"Shouldn't you be in school right now Jed?"

"He is skipping school. I mean he is studying university level classes." Oliver said. "Really"

"Why not. That could not be any weirder than getting sentenced to a year of foster care just because you are seventeen. Have you ever heard of foster care? I would never have imagined such a thing existed."

∞

Marco and his regular gang were sitting more toward the center of the space. One of his buddies remarked there was a new crop of nerds and losers, looking at Oliver, Jed and Babs.

"You are wrong about that particular bunch. The kid is some sort of genius and his brother has been taking care of him since high school. They're orphans. The girl was from that Mormon cult they busted last year. Looks like she had a tough year since. No, that bunch has simply been beaten up unjustly by the demons of fate."

Miley Brady said, "You are too simpatico Marco." and threw a french-fry at him.

"That will cost you on the tatami mats tonight," he scowled.

"Oh shit, should have kept my mouth shut," said Miley both frightened and thrilled at getting the attention of this handsome monster of Jujitsu.

Later that evening, Smiley Miley wasn't smiling. Marco true to his word had pounded her ass to the mats too hard, too many times. The other students were looking side eyed at the whole thing. Finally, the hour was up, and the students were making for the door.

"Miley, please stay afterward. We have a few things more to go over," Marco commanded.

He started going over some of the finer balance details with her until everyone left. He went to the front and locked the door.

"You know why I went so hard on you tonight?" Marco asked.

"Because I threw a French fry at you?"

"That was an excuse. To really be good at Jujitsu, you have to have the discipline to roll with it. Absorb it until the time is right. That takes mental concentration."

"Uh huh," Miley replied wanting to please.

"Let's see if you really can control or your body reacts like it wants. Sit down and pull off the bottoms of the Gi."

Miley, smiling again, did as she was asked. '*This is gonna be good*' she thought without knowing exactly what he was going to do. Her body tensed and shivered a little in anticipation. Marco unwrapped his Gi exposing the powerful upper body of a Jujitsu black belt.

∞

Mosi and Babs were chilling in their dorm room just before mid-term. Babs's hair had grown out some. The roots were healthy, but the rest was still falling apart.

"Mosi, I reserved clippers from the RA would you cut my hair back to zero?" Babs requested her roommate.

"Ordinarily I would refuse on fear of future revenge, but this is probably a good move for you. Go Goth until you get your feet under you again. A little black lipstick, a piercing or two would put your victim past behind you."

"Exactly, you're the best," Babs said with energy, "You know me even though I've clammed up about what happened. Since no good deed goes unpunished, I will tell you about my life up until now. You are going to cry, but I am not as damaged as it is going to sound."

"Let me get the clippers and start while you tell me your tale of woe," Mosi said brightly as she skipped out to the RA's office.

When Mosi got back she went straight into the shearing. Babs told her tale. "Did you know I was raised in a small traditional Mormon community? You know multiple wives and all? Well, I was. Mormons and Navaho have had a long history together. You probably have relatives who are Mormon, so you know some of the stories they whisper. Anyway……"

When Babs had finished Mosi was sitting on the corner of the bed with a horrified expression.

"Brighten up, buttercup. I told you I am not damaged as I should have been. Toward the end at the Olsons, I was in fact manipulating them. I do like sex, and I mean a lot. When they came to talk to me and save my soul, I could make them take me no matter their initial intentions. I hated them so much, forcibly taking me became their punishment."

"Wow, that is messed up," Mosi said.

"What happens is not a victim's fault. But remaining a victim sure is. You are looking at an ex-victim. So many crimes were committed against me, as far as men are concerned, I no longer have rules. My declaration is, I will never have a boyfriend. That is not to say I won't have a boy." Babs thought a moment longer, "Hey, I saw some girls in the shower with earrings in the nipples. Is that piercing and does it make them more sensitive?"

Mosi looked at Babs, off-balance from the new tangent, and answered, "That is one kind of piercing and I heard it does make them more sensitive. So, how is the boys but no boyfriend thing going to work? Practically speaking I mean."

"I don't know yet but it's going to be fun," and they both laughed uproariously.

Mosi got out her makeup kit. "You never put-on makeup in your life, have you?"

"Nope," and they both got the grins again.

∞

After four years of mechanical engineering, Jujitsu, skiing and mountain biking, New Mexico felt very much like home. Then the letter from immigration arrived. His student visa was expiring with his graduation. Marco had a decision to make. Joining the Marines to gain citizenship was a no-brainer. His choice was whether to extend from four to six years and be an officer. If he had just gone through ROTC, then it would have been easier. Officer Candidate School was tough. Marco was a six-foot three mass of muscle. His bulk did not come from lifting weights at the gym.

'What the hell, I am a tough guy.' Marco thought, "Yes, it is the only smart thing to do here." He told the Recruiter.

"Wonderful, now your MOS. Your engineering degree almost guarantees you a job on staff at headquarters." The recruiter said.

"Fuck that, I want a fighting specialty, preferably infantry." Marco declared totally surprised that had come out of his mouth.

The recruiter frowned a little. Engineers were hard to come by. But this guy definitely had the gung-ho spirit of a Marine. It took less than five minutes for the printer to spit all the documents out.

"Sign the pages with the colored tabs. And report to the Albuquerque airport next week." The recruiter in a hurry now that he had sealed the deal. And it was lunch time.

The next five years were very fulfilling for Marco. He gained confidence leading men, the senior staff sent him the newest toys to break because of his engineering skills, and the senior

NCOs regularly schooled him in hand-to-hand combat. Ten years of Jujitsu was not the same as a life and death struggle. Then the Chinese started acting stupid.

∞

Ariel grew up on a ranch in the Red River Valley of western TX. As a child, she always raced to get her chores done. That way she had time to spend with Chuckles, her barrel racing horse. It didn't matter that she would win regional championships but never state. As long as Chuckles was under her, she felt queen of the world. Riding out into the rodeo arena with a flag or charging the barrels in a race pumped her with adrenaline. Boys could never get her cranked up as much as galloping at breakneck speeds on a powerful horse. By the end of high school, Chuckles was too old to push in competition and Ariel didn't have the heart to start on a new horse. That's when she knew those carefree days were almost over. Her Pa wanted her to go to University nearby at Texas Tech, but her Ma knew there was too much tomboy in her, at least for now.

Ariel had grown into five foot nine of lean muscle and sinew. Her breasts remained small because there wasn't an ounce of fat on her. Ranch work did that to girls who were not the frilly and Ariel was definitely the tomboy sort. Her curly red hair was matched by a dense spangle of freckles and deep blue eyes. Nothing got past those intense eyes without being noted.

The day dawned with a swirling of light winds from the air being heated by the sun. An hour earlier when the Pettigrews had gotten up, all was still and a little cool. Ma had fixed a big breakfast to send off Ariel and Pa on what was going to be a long day of vaccinations and branding. The wind pushed Ariel's mass of red curls across her face as they rode north to the far pastures. The cows with the youngest calves were there and they would be the last of this year's crop to be branded. The next cycle of work would be the weaning in the fall. Ariel expected to be elsewhere at that time.

"You sure Manuel and Cisco will be waiting when we get back with these?" Ariel asked Pa just before they got to the gate. "I heard all those guys owed money to the Thompsons and weren't allowed to work on other ranches."

"I don't see how he could keep them. He don't own them and if they do owe money, this is a way they could earn some to pay it back." Her pa replied.

"Just what I heard. The Thompsons are not good folk." Ariel said then broke into a long loud call, "HeeeyyyyUp, HeeeyyyyUp, HeeeyyyyUp."

The cows, used to Ariel, raised their heads and began walking toward the gate. They knew the sound of the girl who brought them salt and hay. When they got to the gate, the girl started shouting at them, whistling too loud and jumping around with her horse until they were out and on the way to the corral. Nothing good happened there, but sooner started, the sooner back.

When the herd got to the ranch compound, Manuel and Cisco were at the corral gate and had the propane fire ring going with the branding irons already getting hot. These Mexican illegals were good workers. They made family ranching possible by their responsible, cheap labor.

"Buenos dias Mr. Lyle, Miss Ariel," Cisco called out.

"Morning boys," Lyle replied. "Good, you have us almost ready to go. Manuel, go work the separation gate while Ariel cuts out the calves. Cisco we'll go set up by the squeeze chute and headgate."

Like a good team, they soon had a rhythm and flow going. Fill the box. Get the calves into the headgate, brand, vaccinate and release. Over and over. They were about two thirds done when Ma rang the dinner bell.

Since it was such a nice day, and the heat of summer was just arriving Ma had laid out a spread on the picnic table under the oak tree. The men stuck their heads under the faucet first because they knew if they let Ariel go before, she would shake her long locks out like a dog, soaking whoever was waiting their turn. When she got to the table everyone waited until she sat before attacking the grub. The Mexican cowboys were pleasant company with polite talk. After everyone had their fill of brisket, potato salad and beans, Cisco brought up the subject of pay.

"Mr. Lyle, could you do us a favor? Instead of paying cash like usual, could you send the money to our families next time you are in town?" Cisco said, "I will write down the information."

"We can't get to town and they need the money we usually send," Manuel added.

"Yes of course. Your working here today won't cause problems for you will it. Ariel said things weren't right over at the Thompsons." Lyle asked.

"This is the only way to get them money, so I don't care if Mr. Thompson throws a fit. I can't say any more." Cisco replied. "We are ready to get back after those calves when you are. Thank you for the wonderful lunch, Mrs. Pettigrew."

They both got up and wandered back to the corral. Lyle's face was grim as he watched them leave.

"I knew those Thompsons were abusing but sounds like it is getting out of hand." He said to no one in particular.

The rest of the day flew by and they were bathing the horses by three. Ariel carried a pitcher of lemonade down to where her Ma and Pa were setting up a shooting table by the fence. Scattered at various distances and angles were the pistol targets. About fifty meters out, Pa had rigged up a chain loop so that the metal targets would pop up for a few seconds in a pseudo random fashion. The Pettigrew family liked to shoot replica weapons. Ariel was using a Winchester 73 lever action rifle. She could hit a target in less than two seconds with the rifle starting from a non-shouldered ready position, every time. Her Pa was shooting with a Colt Peacemaker. Ma was spotting.

"Lyle, I think it's time to go get your eyes checked again.," Ma commented after watching him miss for the third time.

"Ordinarily, I would blow you a big raspberry, but you might be right. Too much Texas sun on these blue eyes. Could be cataracts."

"If you think there is a problem, I can drive you into Lubbock on Monday. You can't be a good Texas Tech Red Raider if you can't get your guns up."

"Whoa there little missy, said I couldn't see the target, not get my guns up."

Ma fell to laughing which progressed to a coughing fit.

"Ma, doesn't look like you are much ahead of Pa," Ariel teased.

"Why don't you come with us. We can take in a matinee. It has been a long time since you were away from the ranch." Pa said.

"You know I am content to stay right here. I'll be fine. Take your daughter to that matinee."

"Let me practice quick draw for a while with the Chiappa Regulator, then we can call it a day." Ariel said.

A box of fifty later she had had enough. No bandidos around these days to square off against anyway.

The next day Lyle Pettigrew spent nearly an hour with the optometrist. When he came out Ariel wasn't there. He waited out in front of the office for ten minutes before he saw her come out of the Navy recruiter's office across the street. With a little bit of sadness, he waited for his only daughter to walk over.

"How are your eyes Pa?"

"Got just a touch of cataracts but it will be five more years before they are a problem. Just needed new glasses," he paused for a moment, "Navy?"

"Yeah, you know I have to do something. I can't be a rancher's wife. Not for a while yet anyway. There is a big world out there."

"What would you do in the Navy?"

"Oh Pa, they have a specialty called the Seabees. Combat construction and demolition. They fight and they build."

"That does sound right for you since Calvary doesn't use horses anymore. Tell me about it dear."

Ma was only a little surprised when Ariel announced she was joining the Navy to see the world. The Navy in its infinite wisdom assigned Ariel to the Seabees with special training in demolition. And thus, began her solid career of blowing shit up, then building something back in its place.

∞

The Covid Pandemic shattered the world's economy. The whipsaw of social isolation, opening the economy followed by another surge in infections followed by, yet another economic closure pushed an already unbalanced economy to collapse. World trade and travel crept to a total standstill. A worldwide depression had started. Smaller companies were swallowed by big mega-corporations who had the money and political backing to be rescued by the various governments. Usually, the workers were not absorbed. They ended on the economic trash heap. The only bright side was global warming had finally stopped.

America and China were already at odds over China's bullying of neighbors, unfair economic practices, stealing intellectual property and outright seizure of its weaker neighbors' economic zones in the South China Sea. When the Chinese military started openly fortifying man-made islands, shooting at passing ships, sinking Philippine and Vietnamese fishing boats, an alliance was formed to push them back to internationally recognized borders. The whole world could see the war coming.

∞

Oliver graduated the same year as the Covid took hold. Their diplomas were emailed to them. With no graduation parties, everyone sat at home wondering what the future would hold. Easy to get depressed in such a situation. Oliver and Jed took it in stride. They had a place to live rent free in Roswell, a little money was still in the bank and he would twist Malcolm's titty for a job.

Malcolm who owned RASP, Roswell Aerospace Scrap and Parts, was partially to blame for the death of Oliver and Jed's father. He had sent him to pick up an airplane he knew was less than marginal. When it crashed on landing in Roswell, he was devastated. Corey was his friend and he left Mildred a widow. Giving a job to a hardworking Oliver was the least he could do. Business for him was actually good since so many planes had been grounded in the new economy.

War

2022

The Chinese runway on Mischief Reef had been mostly knocked out by the combined amphibious assault of US, Vietnamese and Philippine Marines but there were still two regiments of Chinese PLA soldiers dug in and scattered throughout their support base. The Chinese had blocked the two passes into the lagoon by sinking cargo ships sideways in the channel. To be able to root out the bunkers in a reasonable time, heavy armor needed to be put ashore. Landing craft, loaded with tanks, could not make it over the seawall. Enter the Seabees with Ariel Pettigrew in tow. Ariel's hair was now high and tight like the other war fighters. Her shoulders and arms had bulked up too. Much had changed in her life.

"Ok, girls and boys, when we bump up against the seawall, I want to see only assholes and elbows getting the charges off the boat. Seaward side you bunch of dolts. I do not want a stray RPG blowing us to hell. JackJack, you are with me to set the detonators. Jayboy, Sanchez start in the middle and work out fifty kilos every two meters twenty charges on each side. Big badda boom gonna let the big boom boys go boom, boom, boom. Hooyah?" Ariel shouted at her crew over the naval gunfire softening her area of the beach.

"Hooyah" they all shouted back. Suddenly the gunfire went quiet. The huge noise of the props in the open top hovercraft started changing as they slowed down to climb the riprap up to the seawall. Thirty seconds later the craft dropped on her skirts and Seabees boiled over the side.

Ariel got her first charge primed just as the team on her side of the hovercraft finished laying out the second.

"Great job guys keep it up and we will be out of here in five minutes," she shouted.

Four minutes and thirty seconds later the hovercraft was lifting and scrapping back toward the sea.

"Green across the board on mine," Jackson reported.

"Mine too. Slave yours to mine and we are good to go," She said. "Done. Just a little farther out to get some safe separation. Oh crap."

"What?"

Ariel just pointed at the machine gun crew setting up in a crater a couple of hundred meters down the beach. The hovercraft was already maxed out when the rounds started chewing them up. A flurry of rounds hit the engines and the hovercraft went silent as they settled in the water.

"All the separation we are gonna get in this life. Fire in the hole, fire in the hole." Ariel shouted and actioned the detonators.

A huge explosion along the seawall turned it into a gravel ramp seventy meters wide. Several large chunks also tore through the Seabees hovercraft already full of machine gun holes. Ariel looked around and all but two of her men were dead. Both of those had been hit. She started first aid and hoped the medivac would arrive soon enough. The machine gunners started having trouble of their own. Small favors.

∞

Gen. Frank of the US Air Force walked into Chief Petty Officer Pettigrew's hospital room and was surprised to find Captain Rocha there as well. Fresh flowers were in a vase and a box of chocolates on the nightstand.

"Well, this is fortuitous. I was looking for both of you. I am Gen. Frank USAF. How are you Chief?"

Ariel was lying in bed with a sheet pulled up to her chin. She replied, "Tired of this place. I don't have survivors' guilt like the doctors say I should have. What I got is itchy feet."

"Want to get out of here, I'm buying."

Ariel threw the sheet back and hopped to the floor. She was fully dressed down to her boots.

"Marc...um, Captain Rocha was going to spring me but a General is so much better. Let's go"

They walked down the hall to the exit. The doctors did not notice their patient escaping. It didn't take long for them to find a servicemen's bar just outside the Ho Chi Minh City hospital. It was decorated in retro 1968 complete with the smell of marijuana. The General ordered a pitcher of beer.

"It may seem unconventional for me to be picking your brains on a potential operation, but I have seen staff officers kill too many men too easily. Call this research before inter-service cooperation. You two have done what I need doing. Under fire. Staff officers don't get that their pretty Power Points are real lives."

"What are the objectives?" Captain Marco Rocha asked getting straight to the point.

Gen. Frank pulled out a recon photo showing the Chinese base on Fiery Cross Reef. He pointed to near the middle of the runway where there was a large flight apron.

"I want to operate a squadron of Air Force A-10s and Marine Apaches from this area for the purpose of close air support in taking the base surrounding it. This will be a mostly Vietnamese ground show, but I want Americans turbocharging its allies."

"Wow, the infantry is going to love that but the pilots and weapons techs not so much," Marco said.

"Exactly, which is where you two come in."

"You need to blow the seawall here near the athletic field for hovercraft to bring in armor straight to the apron, followed by dozers to push up a berm. Blow the seawall on the opposite side of the runway to allow a one-way flow." Ariel said seeing the solution.

"I agree," Marco said. "Armor pushes them away while the dozers get started. The armor needs support by a company of Marines to clear, then hold the perimeter. Afterward, the dozers would be damned useful in clearing the rest of the base. We learned that lesson in the street fight of Mosel taking out ISIS."

"See how smart I am," beamed Gen. Frank. "Just got to know who to ask. Now let's talk about some details to make this go."

The three then hatched out a plan that would be studied in military academies for a century. They also got pretty drunk on beer.

∞

Ariel was thinking, *'how the hell did I get myself into the same situation... Again.'* It was someone else's team this time, but she was there listening to the same sort of pre-action pep talk as she had given a month ago. Even the same model of hovercraft. A few minutes passed and they rode up the riprap and sat on their skirt. Over the top. This time they would stay ashore. The Marines had captured a toe hold in the nearby buildings.

Chief Petty Officer's Dupre's team worked fast too. Not as good as her's but good enough. Five minutes and ten seconds for the same size stretch. Over the seawall and into the first building for cover. Kaboom. Not bad, good ramp. The following hovercraft were one minute out when the Navy's prep bombardment began destroying everything alongside the coming route of the hovercraft loaded with armor and Marine infantry.

'Marco would be in that first wave. God, I hope he is not killed' Ariel thought. *'If he, if we survive, I am going to marry that jarhead.'*

The assault hovercraft sped by the Seabee demolition team. There would be a Vietnamese team to blow the seawall on the opposite side across the runway. The hovercraft could slide up to the runway apron discharge and keep going back to sea. That was the plan. Of course, the enemy always has a say in the plan.

∞

The Havoc Marco was in got dumped off at the intersection just past the athletic field. The Chinese had been caught flat footed again and only small arms fire pinged against the armor. The 40 mm auto-cannon gunner chewed up the corner of the nearest building killing anybody there and creating ingress for the infantry. The driver of his Havoc pulled up to the broken walls and Marco with his team stormed into the building. Another Havoc had done similar work on the corner down the street. This would be Marco's CP for the initial assault. Clearing the building took less than ten minutes. The techs quickly got the antennas on the roof and laptops connected with the platoon leaders. Good news was not the first thing Marco received.

The Marines were making good way in clearing the buildings facing the runway but the APC carrying the Vietnamese demolition team to the far seawall had been hit by a Red Arrow, a man portable anti-armor rocket. Half were dead, the other half were combat ineffective. The second APC with most of the explosives had made it to the wall and the crew was feverishly throwing charges over the wall as fast as possible under small arms fire. This was going to foul up the flow of following waves if the hovercraft couldn't travel straight back to sea.

"I need Dupre's team to the opposite seawall as soon as possible." Marco was talking to the Colonel in charge of the beachhead at the first seawall. "I will stop hovercraft 37. Unload the Havocs there, stuff Dupre's team into one and send it straight across. The explosives are there. They just need demolition experts. Send the rest of the Havocs to the apron and start clearing east. Advise them there are some Red Arrow crews working that area."

"HC 37, HC 37, Rocks actual," Marco called on the radio.

"HC 37 go ahead."

"I need you to discharge just past the breach and return to sea same way."

"Understood, Havocs discharged at breach return same."

46

∞

"Dupre, I need your team aboard a Havoc that will be here shortly. Second team got hit crossing the runway." Col. Rankin ordered over the radio. "We will empty a Havoc at the breach. Get aboard and haul ass to the other side. If we don't get an exit route open soon, the pile up will be a target for a ballistic missile strike.

Jacques Dupre was assembling his men when a mortar round landed at his feet. Every one of his team died. Ariel had not rounded the corner of the building yet. Carnage was spread out in front of her and flashbacks of her own team started hammering her psyche. Col. Rankin's aide showed up at her side a moment later.

"Damn, damn, damn" was all he could say. Ariel took a few steps away and puked the lunch she had just eaten. A lunch that had saved her life. The extra minute to scrap up the last of the cheese sauce had put her around the corner from this.

"Dupre, Dupre they are waiting. Where the fuck are you?" Col. Rankin was yelling over the radio.

Ariel keyed her mike, "Dupre and his whole team are dead. Tell the Havoc driver I will be there in thirty seconds." Ariel grabbed Dupre's rucksack with the detonator controls and sprinted toward the breach.

"Where is the rest of the team," the driver asked as Ariel jumped in.

"All dead. It's just me, so haul ass. This situation needs to get un-fucked, soonest."

His reply was brief, "Yes Ma'am" The trip to the other side was brief as well. They rocketed straight ahead and went the one km distance to the wall in a minute and ten seconds. The driver skidded up to the wall, Ariel bailed out the back and leapt over the seawall. She landed three meters from two Chinese soldiers who were heaping up the charges on a piece of canvas so they could drag them away. Everyone was completely surprised and then they weren't. Everyone went for their gun at the same time, but Ariel's hours of practice won. She popped both in the face with her 9mm before they could bring up their long guns. A lifetime of farm work enabled her to scatter charges along the seawall embedding detonators as she went. Time to go.

She sprinted one hundred meters to the east and just around a slight bend. Kaboom and another breach was made. Hovercraft props were cranking up again. Ariel sat down with her back to the seawall looking out to sea. For a few minutes she was racked by sobbing, thinking about her lost team and Dupre's.

Marco came over the radio, "Great work Ariel. Just stay there for now. We will mop up here and send an APC in a couple of hours to pick you up. You have done more than your bit."

"I am happy staying here" she replied.

Marco had a very busy two hours. There was so much confusion in the half rubble, half whole buildings in front of the apron he had to go see to the disposition of his platoons. A couple of times an enemy soldier popped out of a door and had to be dispatched in hand to hand fighting. Marco was covered in the blood of his enemies. He started to feel charged with a battle fever.

One of his butter bar lieutenants had completely lost it. He had scattered his squads in such a way they were in each other's firing line. And then froze as fifty Chinese Marines started pushing forward hard. Not trying to find cover, hold and fire, the Chinese Marines were dodging from point to point firing constantly. Marco was a couple hundred meters away when he saw it happen. If those fifty were to get among his armor, the assault would fail.

"Laurel bring your SAW, Henry grab that box of ammo and follow me," Marco shouted. He finally overrode the lieutenant's radio and pulled the forward squad out of the line of fire as he and his fire team raced to a pile of rubble beside the beleaguered platoon. Laurel started laying down the suppressing fire as Henry and Marco picked off any Chinese shooting back at their little fire base. All three were completely in the open but there was nothing for it. Take the chance or lose the fight. Laurel keep up a withering fire and the Chinese lost forty men. The remainder decided to pull back and the immediate crisis was averted.

Good as his word, a couple of hours later a Havoc pulled up near Ariel, "Someone call for a taxi?" the same driver as before shouted. A few rounds of small arms fire pinged on the armor as they crossed the runway to the Apron where dozers were already pushing up sand berms to protect the flight line crews. Marco was shaking the hand of a Vietnamese colonel and directed her toward a hovercraft disgorging Vietnamese Marines. Armor had made the initial incision, but the rest of the fight was going to be a close quarters brutality.

"What's up?" Ariel asked.

"Gen. Frank has ordered us both back to the Amphibious Dock. Said our mission was accomplished."

"I won't argue with that order."

The ride out to the dock was forty minutes but the hovercraft made it too loud to talk so they sat and looked at each other. Just before they pulled into the landing well, Ariel got up, went to sit on Marco's lap and gave him a long deep kiss. Then she shouted in his ear, "I am going to marry you."

Marco shouted back, "Yes, you are."

Somehow, they arrived in Marco's quarters and fell together for the most intense, wild sex either had ever had.

Quantum of Roswell

Jed had maintained contact with a professor from his time at New Mexico Tech. "Dr. Lee I have been thinking," Jed started and then stared off into space.

Merry now used to the young protégé, waited patiently. After five minutes, Jed restarted, "If we use a higher temperature, say around 1400 degrees Kelvin, then the production of entangled quantum pairs is huge. Using an electric field to separate the pairs as they flow by, we can grow crystals to be much bigger. The twins will be less well arranged in the crystal lattice but also more stable. Using an error correcting recursive coding scheme, we can work around the irregular placement in the crystal lattice of each of the twins. The crystal will be bigger but more tunable over a longer time."

"And what material were you thinking? "

Jed got the same faraway look again. Dr. Merry went to make coffee and get comfortable.

"Strontium sulfate. That's kind of ironic since Celestine, the mineral it comes from is used in fireworks which were one of the earliest forms of communications at a distance."

Merry just smiled and said "The rock physics lab has some strontium sulfate. Let's go get some and set up an experiment "

An hour later, the sulfate was bubbling gas in a retort, the natural pressure of boiling caused a slow flow through an improvised electric field which split the quantum entangled pairs into two separate chambers. A tiny flake of Celestine of the pale blue variety was used as the seed. Dr. Lee watched the crystals growing more slowly than the eye could perceive.

"Hurry up, damn it," he said with a chuckle.

"They may hear you, but they won't understand." Jed said without looking up from his tablet where he was writing a long complex string of equations with a stylus. "What if we were a hundred light years away and the crystal suddenly shouts, 'Hurry up damn it.' Wouldn't we be surprised?"

"If you get a hundred light years away, give me a call to let me know how it's going."

"OK," Jed replied, "You never know when you need to phone home, just like E.T. "

"This is going to take a while. I'll take you back to Roswell. We can try it out next week." Dr. Lee s

∞

The following week, Dr Lee showed up in Roswell with two pale blue orthorhombic crystals. Jed attached them to the two devices that looked extremely simple.

"Those look like Marconi's original invention," Dr. Lee said a bit irritated.

"Not exactly," Jed replied "I am using focused microwaves not sound waves. Sound is too low a frequency to have any bandwidth. Modulated microwaves passing thru one causes change in both twins. The microwave signal after passed through now contains how its twin was modulated as well as its local signal. Subtract local known input and you have input from the twin. To test them for the real-world needs separation because it is too easy to have crosstalk and if it can't go the distance, what's the point. We can get a simple radio tuned to the time service; you know the one with the atomic clock tick. Put one set in a box and mail it to say Australia. We modulate our local crystal side-by-side with another atomic clock and see if they drift. Do you have a colleague that can receive them and send them back afterwards? "Jed asked.

"That is an incredibly elegant solution. Yes, I do know someone at Curtin University actually. Well, let's run down to Radio HamBone and spend two hundred on a billion-dollar invention."

"Can I stay here? That place gets crowded. "

"Of course, my boy. I'll just be an hour and we can play some more."

The Q comm finally arrived in Perth. Professor Romansky unpacked it, plugged mains power and then tuned the radio to the local atomic clock service.

"I wonder what that crazy hippie is up to now?" Romansky muttered to himself. He then sent a text to Dr. Lee letting him know everything was live.

Merry Lee looked at his text, grunted and went back to sleep. He had started logging data before going to bed.

The next morning while sipping coffee he reviewed the data. They were exact whether coming through the Australia Q comm set or directly from a local time service. Looking at the time he called his friend. Romansky picked up on the first ring.

"Well did it work?"

"Seems to be very solid. Zero lag. Do me another favor and plug a headset into the device, I want to hear the quality of voice. A few minutes later and they were talking on the set.

"This is better than a landline. Quantum sets are usually very noisy." Romansky said.

"There is a Wi-Fi in the box. Let's see how Skype video looks."

When his buddy came up on the video, the feed was very good.

"When you get ready to sell some of these, I want to be first in line." Romansky said.

After hanging up, Dr. Lee and Jed started working on the patent application. The main problem was theft by the mega-corporations. Corporations had entire teams watching patent applications for things they could make some small change to and claim as their own. Too much detail and they could reproduce it. Too little detail and the patent was worthless. Their legal teams and ownership of the political process insured impunity. The Chinese, of course, just copied it and legalities be damned.

Dr. Lee and Jed took a third route. They were vague about what it could do in the English description but rigorous in the mathematical. Very few people could follow the high-level calculations, certainly not the corporate weanies. Jed was listed as the inventor as well as the assignee. Oliver would probably be the one to take it commercial, hopefully they would not link him to the patent. At least long enough to be able to defend themselves.

"We need to get some commercial off the shelf tech to go around these. Something where we can use the Q comm as trunks and feed them with regular cell calls, maybe radio too," Dr. Lee said, "That way we could make use of their abilities without risking exposure of our tech."

Gravitas

Oliver finally cut through the wing root and there came a tremendous crash as the wing hit the concrete. Malcolm would not be pleased. Malcolm be damned, fuel was spraying, and any spark would be the end of Oliver.

"Damn it, that tank should have been empty," Oliver muttered as he switched off his cutter.

"About time," Malcolm's voice sneered from the radio. "If that plane isn't in its major pieces by end of day, we'll have to revisit our arrangement."

"And then you'll have to hire someone who wouldn't call the Fire Department every time one of your regular idiots leave fuel in the tanks. Better get someone over here before there's a plume of smoke you can see in downtown Roswell. About 300 liters of jet fuel is spreading out"

"Shit"

"What you want me to do now?" Oliver asked.

"I guess you can finish the day helping Lenny pull engines. Can you come in tomorrow? Got an aluminum order next week I can't miss."

"Fine, but I'll need a 3-hour lunch break. Gotta thing on with Jed and his professor."

"We'll make it work," Malcolm replied before going back to his magazine.

∞

"Howdy Jed. Make any breakthroughs on your idea today?" No answer. "Jed?" No answer. Looking in the fridge. "Jed, you didn't eat the lunch I fixed you."

Oliver sighing sat down next to his brother putting his arm around Jed's bicep gently squeezing and pulling back until his pencil left the notebook.

"Oh!!! Hi, didn't hear you come in," Jed said a little startled.

"I know."

"Think I found a way to measure gravity waves directly. Going to need some rare earth magnets though. Hey, what are you going doing home so early?" Jed asked.

"It's 6:30 bro," Oliver said gently.

"Oh sorry, I was so into this didn't pay attention. Man, I'm hungry"

"Dinner will be ready in about forty-five minutes. Do not get into those Cheetos."

∞

The next day Dr. Meriwether Lee, professor of Astrophysics at New Mexico Institute of Mining and Technology, had come to visit his prodigy.

"Are you seeing any errors Dr. Lee?" Jed asked.

"Not yet, if this takes us where I think, then it's huge. Give me an hour of solitude Jed. Go jogging, get something to eat, take a shower, go relax," Dr. Lee mumbled making a shooing motion without looking up.

Jed headed out the door to do exactly what he was told by his mentor. Oliver looked up from making lunch and asked his brother where he was going. Since the food was almost ready.

"Dr. Lee told me to go run. Then I can eat. He can't seem to look up from my ideas."

Oliver chuckled "Half an hour about right?"

"Uh huh."

Dr Lee's brain was on fire with the implications. The simple, but savant boy, not old enough to shave had just come up with a practical gravity manipulation concept and had the mathematical proof to back it up. Dr Lee didn't need an hour to check the equations, he needed a decade to figure out what would happen next, a Nobel Prize, or a CIA prison. Exactly thirty minutes later, Jed came into the kitchen and let the screen door bang behind him. Dr. Lee hearing the door stumbled in from the living room in a daze.

"Hey Dr. Merry, you're going to eat with us. We have plenty," Oliver said.

"Sure, sure," Dr. Lee absent mindedly replied, staring like a laser at the skinny kid who just turned the world on its head.

"Jed, Oliver, we need to have a very serious discussion. Part now, the rest later after some thought. Because if the experiment works out, and the creek don't rise, the world will be changed within a couple of years. It changes for us today."

"Jed?" Oliver said looking at his brother.

"Gravity manipulation. I think we can come up with parts in the boneyard to make it work."

Roswell Boneyard

"No shit!!!"

"That's all you have to say, no shit?" Dr. Lee asked.

"Well, he is Jed, but you're right, if we can build something that's practical, the world would change," Oliver declared.

∞

Over the next month Oliver found the material needed in the vast piles of scrap that was the Roswell aircraft boneyard. When aircraft were to be scrapped, not mothballed, they came here. Twenty men working off and on, removed working engines, dismantled major parts, and fed most of it to the shredder. The more rare, expensive alloys and elements found a different pile than the sheet aluminum and insulation. Copper, rare earth elements, even junk turbofan blades got their own final resting pile. Electronic systems, boards, antennas, and whatever might have a used part value, had a warehouse bin to reside in.

Graphene had become a holy grail, but piece by piece Oliver amassed thirty sq. meters to go with his twenty kg of rare earth magnets. Time to assemble the first cell. It took Jed and Oliver the best part of a week to press the layers and mask the semi-conductor coils to have a four hundred sq. cm cell.

"Ok, so we apply a thirty volts DC directly through the cell and forty-five volts at the earth's microseism frequency through the coils." Jed directed.

"Right, it's dialed in. Sure you don't want a ramp up?" Oliver asked.

"Naw. A simple switch won't hurt anything at these voltages, and I didn't see anything in the physics where it made a difference."

"Switching on now," Oliver said as he hit the relay button then immediately shouted, "Look out!!"

A hole had suddenly appeared in the roof of the hanger and years of dirt and debris started raining down.

"Oops," giggled Jed, "maybe we should turn the base current down a little."

"But hot damn!" Oliver jumped up and spun his brother into a hug. "It works, damn does it work!"

"Well of course. Although the output is much stronger than I calculated. Maybe by a factor of ten," Jed replied with a faraway look.

After a few minutes Jed resumed his thoughts, "You know, this result is using only four- and two-layer graphene sheets. If we used four- and six-layer sheets, then we could do a lot more to form the gravity field, not just a simple vectoring."

"What do you mean?" Oliver quizzed.

"This is good for a grav sled, ground vehicle or creating a fun room with zero G, but to make something fly independently, we need to have one of the layers as six plies. Four and six, even better, as it will give very good control to make shapes. I would not have known that were possible without this experiment though." Jed explained.

"We do have three square meters of six plies in pieces of different sizes. Some of it is not in very good shape."

"That could be enough to do a first test but if it is too brittle then it will break up before very much use," Jed said after a few minutes thought.

"Crawl before we run brother."

"Something else that I think is going to be important is the formation of a bubble. With the six-four solution, a bubble will be formed. Inside that bubble, there will be no inertia so the whole system can be accelerated at multiple Gees without the internal area feeling it."

"Crap," Oliver said.

"I thought you would like that."

"I do, too much. Now I need to find a good source of six plies. You realize if we can accelerate constantly with no felt effect, we can zoom to the moon in hours, or the asteroid belt in a few days," Oliver said feeling his heart race.

"That is why I brought it up," Jed smiled shyly.

∞

The following weeks were a blur. When Oliver was not working for Malcolm, he and Jed were assembling layers of graphene, rare earth magnets and semi-conductor coils, putting them under the stamping machine and pressing the shit out of them. It was difficult getting all these disparate materials to bond at a molecular level.

They now had fifty cells spread out and placed five cells per panel into sleeves welded into the lower frame curvature of an old military transport. The tedious task of seeing how the cells interacted began.

"Throw another bucket of sand, and then we'll do another LIDAR." Dr. Lee said.

After five buckets per shape and 20 iterations, they were starting to get more than a few inches built up on the hanger floor. The Lidar units kicked on in the roof joists and measured one more shape, made of sand held in the gravity field.

"We got a lot of data that will need to be reduced," Oliver observed.

"Know any good data processors?" Dr. Lee asked.

"I know a good coder. Her name is Babs," Oliver said, "And let me tell you about Babs."

Oliver started his story. "She has been working for a contractor at Sandia Labs who are supporting JPL on deep and near space navigation. Extraordinary woman, very sharp with code and sexy as hell. The sexy part is why everyone, guys at least, remember her. One time that I saw her in action burned into my memories forever. I was just finishing my first freshman year at Tech and had taken a date down to the Owl for green chili cheeseburgers. I AM cheap but the place is famous for them. Anyway, we sat at a table against the wall near the bar. She was there with a couple of girls at the next table talking about some programming stuff. I knew her pretty well at the time, but since I was with a date, I simply smiled and nodded my head. She did the same. The waitress had just brought our burgers when I hear one of the girls say "Oh Shit. That's Tom at the bar. What an asshole, dumped me when I wouldn't put out on the second date." So, Babs says, "If I embarrass him to your satisfaction will you buy tonight?" The other girl laughs and says, "Let's see what you got."

So, Babs walks over to Tom, who is on a stool at the bar, reaches around and grabs his forearms. The look on his face was like a deer in headlights. And then Babs purrs to him "Don't move for five minutes and you'll get lucky tonight." The guy grins a shit eating grin and says "OK". Babs starts brushing her breasts on his back, breathing and kissing on the side of his neck while slowly stroking one of his forearms on the bar. The other hand is inside his shirt doing something. We could see the guys face in the mirror behind the bar slowly twisting up in pleasure. This went on for maybe 3 minutes when suddenly he got a surprised look. Babs backs off says "Oh sorry," went back to her table and started eating her burger. The guy had creamed his jeans leaving a huge stain. His buddies fell off their stools laughing. Poor Tom of course bolted for the door. The other girl told Babs "You win," and they went back to discussing Fortran. That was Babs at her finest."

"I know Miss Whiting," responded Dr. Lee. "Good story though."

"This is looking like the barge can be flown to wherever we want. Our Q comm works for controls, but one big problem I can see is to power it. A big enough battery is not really in my budget." Oliver said.

"We have a little time. A solution will appear," Dr. Lee said confidently.

∞

At her standing desk Babs was finally finding where the nested do loop was getting hung up when she felt a presence behind her. Dr. Farseian, a short fat bald man, the chief scientist on the project, began massaging her shoulders.

"You need to relax some," he cooed.

"You need to stop breaking my concentration. And stop touching me!" Babs said tossing her shoulder.

"I figured with your past, a little massage, even a hug would be welcome," Farseian continued and moved closer.

"My past is my own and if I feel your genitals brush me, they will get so damaged you'll truly understand the Blue Screen of Death."

"Fine," he said backing off. "Did you find the cause of your program crashes?"

"I did and was formulating a fix when you interrupted,"

As Farseian went on his way looking for someone else to harass, Babs mumbled under her breath, "Fuck this place, fuck this place."

∞

"Hi Babs, this is Oliver we went to school together at Tech."

"Oh, hi Oliver, it's been a long time. How have you and Jed been getting along?" she replied.

"Truthfully, just scraping by."

"Yeah, like everyone else these days."

"I have a business proposition for you, but I don't want to talk over the phone. Do you suppose we can get together this weekend? You would have to come to Roswell. I can pay the plane ticket."

"Ooomft, a mystery. As it turns out, I plan on quitting my job soon. Fuck it, I can drive down tomorrow and be there at noon." Babs decided on the spot.

"Decisive as always. By the way, Dr. Meriwether Lee is involved. You OK with him?"

"I love old Merry Lee."

"We will be at the old air base boneyard Hanger 13," Oliver informed.

"Hangar 13 seems appropriate for a mystery. See you tomorrow."

Babs hung up and thought about Oliver. A little too serious, but very good at eating pussy. Yes, this might work out.

∞

Marco took the last brick of antibiotics and slid it into the sleeve of his harness.

Pinto Loco, a deathly pale, meth head looked up, "Don't know why you won't take a load of Meth. Pays twice as much and it's the same work." Grinning with a black stump grin he added, "It's hard time either way."

"Got my reasons and it's not either way. It's a third of the time, if I get caught," Marco shot back.

"Yeah whatever, just leave it at the normal drop," Pinto Loco muttered losing focus on the business at hand.

"Later" Marco called as he pulled silently out into the hot, black night on his electric dirt bike.

Stopping a couple of kilometers from the border he pulled out his microdrone and tossed it into the air for the first of many times of the run.

"Let's see where you pendejos left me a gap," Marco muttered as he commanded a grid search and relaxed while watching on his HUD.

Scout, run and stop, over and over brought Marco rolling into Las Cruces at daylight. Another hour of observation confirmed his drop point was safe.

Sighing as he closed the door on an old shed, "Well now just need to get the payment. That will shut up Ariel. That and my dick in her mouth."

Snickering and enjoying the morning now that the immediate danger was passed, Marco cruised toward his pickup truck and a well-deserved nap.

∞

Good as her word, Babs arrived at Hanger 13 around noon. The three-hour drive from Albuquerque gave time to reflect about the environment with her current employer and what working in a startup company might bring. She obviously needed a change and a hope for something better out of life. Her conclusion was 'nothing ventured nothing gained'.

Oliver led her into the hanger past a big frame that looked like the belly hacked out of an old airplane supported by four posts welded to the corners. A cable from the inside of the junk led ten meters over to a table with various notebooks, power supplies and black boxes. Sand was everywhere.

"I hope my job won't be pushing a broom, 'cause you definitively need to do that," Babs said.

"You are right, but that is a feature not a bug. Have a seat let me get things powered up. A demo will be much better than an explanation. Here comes my brother Jed and Dr. Lee," Oliver said.

"Dr. Lee, it's been a while. You look good. Still teaching?" Babs greeted the boys.

"Miss Whiting, hello and welcome to Wonderland. I was declared Professor Emeritus last year, so my time is my own now. They pretend to pay me to do research, but it is just a cheap retirement while staying on the faculty roles. Suits me because I have time to spend with this brilliant young man. Have you met Jed before?"

"Hi Jed. Wow, you grew up nice. Not that skinny kid anymore. We have met. In fact, Jed and Oliver were some of the first friends I made arriving at Tech. You remember my hair?"

"I remember you, Babs. Your hair was funny. That's why I noticed you. That and your eyes," Jed replied.

"Ok, I have the demo ready to go. Let's show it and then go for lunch. She will need time to accept what we have here before talking more seriously," Oliver said.

Oliver started the program and the frame slowly lifted off the ground and hovered. Changing a couple of parameters caused the frame to make a circular route then move up and down by a meter. It was stationary a meter off the ground when Babs finally got control of her jaw and pulled her mouth closed.

"Tell me that is not just magnetic levitation," Babs demanded.

"That is not magnetic effect. It is gravitational," Dr. Lee replied. "We can pack all the controls onboard with a decent battery and fly to the moon if we want."

"Holy shit!" Babs managed to say, then she blurted out, "I don't need a salary just take me with you."

"Ok then, let's go," Oliver said.

"What?" Babs asked with a million thoughts jetting through her mind.

"Yeah, I'm starved," Jed put in, "Oliver promised fried chicken. He said it was your favorite."

Dr. Lee just laughed as he pulled on his coat.

∞

"Sorry we are not wining and dining you, but we are kind of broke," Oliver said between bites of his fast-food chicken.

"It's all right. I really do love this chicken and with a little effort we can get a bunch of money without selling out," Babs declared through her secret recipe drool.

"What is your idea?" Oliver asked.

"Asteroids. I have been working out orbital mechanics for the JPL and know where there are good prospects relatively close. Bet that chopped up plane belly can go get us some," Babs responded. "Biggest problem will be control. The flight paths are easy, but to grab the rocks we will have too long a time lag for remote control."

"We have something to take the lag out entirely. It has enough bandwidth to give us video, some sensors and local control of say an articulating arm," Dr. Lee added. "Our young genius, Jed, came up with decent quantum communications last year. It is still a little shaky but solid enough for this."

"I've got a little money saved if it would help," Babs offered.

"Paying to work. Now that is what I call a good candidate." Oliver said in amusement. "No just some hard work and no pay until we all get our pay day. The Boneyard will provide."

$$\infty$$

"The data will need an inversion. We have the X, Y, Z and G for the different current modulation to elements. We need to create a generalized model so we can drive the G field as we need it. Right now, our data only has values for a single modulation. As you know, different modulations have different outcomes. First things first. Let us get our model and architecture for input manipulation, then we will expand on our experiment," Dr. Lee explained. "And after all that, we know there will be changes as we move the point in the G field that is, as we move about."

"Is that all? No don't answer that," Babs said pensively. "After the mathematical system is resolved then you're going to need a good GUI to run it."

"Yes exactly. How long until you get a first-order approximation?"

"Something solid but simple, in about a month... But, I think it will never truly be done. This will be a living project," Babs declared. "We will need ongoing recording and processing. This is a perfect environment for artificial intelligence, but that increases the IT demands by an order of magnitude. I might know a guy. Ya know whad I mean?" Babs put on her best gangster face.

Their battery problem was solved much more easily and cheaply than Oliver expected. Babs had the simple idea of renting two Telemarks and pulling their batteries. Barge gets back, reinstall batteries and return the cars. Two hundred dollars and they rented thirty thousand dollars of energy storage.

∞

"We have a house on Elm street. Three bedrooms and a large, detached garage. Since we can't pay you yet, you can live with us. That sound good?" Oliver asked.

"Yea, I couldn't pay rent anyway. I thought I was going to sleep on a cot in the hanger. A real house is great. You still have that Camaro?" Babs was pleased she wouldn't be living under a bridge.

"Of course. I don't drive it too often now as it is even more of a classic. Could make a lot of money if I sold it. We could go cruise the Sonic if you are into it? "

"Not much of a Sonic person myself. Keep the car, I think we are going to have a ton of money soon," she said.

A little boneyard engineering would prove her right.

First Flight

Oliver matched the rock's movement to get zero Delta V at three meters away. Jed controlled the grappling arm to slowly swing over and grab the half meter diameter asteroid.

 "Got any magnetism, Jed?" Oliver asked.

"Yeah, pretty strong. Over half iron I bet," he replied.

"I see another, at six kilometers, two twenty degrees azimuth and ten degrees declination. Strong return, probably M-type as well," Babs supplied.

"We're getting heavy. I'll do another mass calculation when we boost over," Dr. Lee advised.

"That last one must have been three hundred kilos by itself. We're already pushing two tons. The next will have to be the last." Jed said.

"I don't want to push our luck much longer on the quantum link either," Oliver said. "The radio works but it is slow and shines a spotlight on us with emissions. Remember, we don't exist."

"OK, I'm secure, let's move; give me zero point one gees for thirty seconds."

"Zero point one coming up in three, two, one mark."

Capturing the last asteroid was the easiest yet. They were coming together as a team and each was getting better at their controls.

"Lay in the program to give us a nice Burrowing polar orbit about one thousand kilometers elevation. Come in from above the elliptical so a polar orbit makes sense if anybody spots us arriving. There is no point in rushing." Oliver requested.

"Okay, done," Babs said.

"No way," Oliver sputtered.

"I knew what you were going to want, so I calculated it while you were scratching your nut sack."

"Okay smart ass how many passes will we have next Saturday night between 10:00 and 4:00?"

"Don't know but when I tweak the approach in a couple of days, I'll get us three chances to land."

"South to North," Jed started giggling. "Drug traffickers are using ballistic missiles now."

"Better than Space Force thinking we are Russian nukes," Dr. Lee said.

∞

Oliver and Jed watched the flow coming down from the rock crusher cylinder. They had decided that selling small pieces would be less suspicious and they needed finer pieces to look for gems. They had already picked up a couple of dozen 3 to 5 caret stones of a clear light blue quality. Just then three stones the size of quail eggs went by. Oliver snatched him up before Jed could blink.

"Now we have a risk and reward situation. These are going to make quite a stir." Oliver declared.

"They are worth how much?" Jed asked.

"The New Yorkers will tell us, but maybe we should spread these three around in Asia. That way it will take a few months before the market realizes there is a new supply of highest quality. It will give us time to create distance. This kind of money will draw out the pirates of all stripes."

∞

"They are worth how much?" Oliver asked again as the broker picked up one of the three carat stones for a third look. The nervous excitement on the man's face was impossible to hide even though a veteran dealer.

"You must know these six matched stones are extraordinary," the dealer queried.

"I do, but I'm also looking for extraordinary discretion," Oliver said emphatically. "You can see they're not blood diamonds, but my source must be protected."

"I can give you top dollar per carat, which is around $30,000. That could double if I could find a larger center stone of the same or better quality to make a matched necklace. Problem is these are such high quality finding other larger to match is, I think, impossible."

"Understood, but it just so happens" Oliver laid a matching eight-carat stone on the mat from his pocket.

Ben Cohen's mouth fell open and he sat back heavily in his chair "How?"

"If you can be discreet then I can get you this same quantity of similar stones once a month, except for the larger one. Can you handle that much? I have a variety of one to five carats."

"Yes, I can and yes I will be. Thinking of the future right now, I can give you $2.5 million for this lot."

"Done," Oliver replied and offered the special handshake of a diamond broker to seal the deal. "Now let's talk about bullion."

"You are kidding?" Ben asked incredulously.

"Quite serious. It will not be industrially made so an assay will have to be done. Expect around ninety-five percent purity on Gold, Platinum, Rhodium and Palladium."

"Did a giant meteorite land in your duck pond?"

This startled Oliver and it took him a moment to compose himself. "Mr. Cohen, it is imperative you do not ask the antecedence of this material. It is not illegal, but how we came in possession is highly sensitive."

"I touched a nerve, my apologies. We are absolutely discrete, but the unusual combination piqued my curiosity," Ben apologized, "The Palladium would be better suited to an industrial client, but the other three interests me. What kind of quantities are we speaking about?"

"Sixty kilos of gold, twenty each of platinum and rhodium. More or less each month." Oliver replied.

Ben inhaled his own spit and started coughing.

"You ok?"

Ben held up one finger. In a moment he said, "You are a very interesting man Mr. Eversole. This is industrial quantities, yet you do not have that air about you. My group of friends is quite large. We can absorb these quantities, but someone will be asking questions especially when the chemistry reveals a non-standard source. Help me, help you."

Knowing this same scene would arise with any other buyer, Oliver decided to take a chance. He needed long term partners to get off the ground. The Jewish community has very broad reach across the globe. They were also used to staying out of the eye of local governments.

"We are mining asteroids," Oliver admitted.

A full minute ticked away before he replied, "I was expecting Antarctica. No more questions from me but please be careful with your other business inquires. The wolves have returned to the world of business like in evil times of the past," He paused again. "The stones are like no other I've seen on earth, but we will scatter them around the world. A little mystery will play well with this clientele. Send me a sample of the metals and I will help you mask their unusual origin."

Oliver pulled slender fingers of each type metal and laid on the counter.

"What no rabbits," Ben asked with a chuckle looking at Oliver's pocket.

"It was a long walk back from the Belt, so we ate them." Oliver said with a grin.

To which Ben roared in laughter. The nervous tension finally got the better of him.

∞

Malcolm looked up as Oliver came into his office, clean for a change. Before Oliver could open his mouth, Malcolm said, "I can't afford to be giving out raises."

Oliver looked back and replied, "Maybe I can."

"What you mean?"

"I am interested in buying Roswell Aerospace Scrap and Parts. It so happens I won the lottery. Work is something fundamental for me, but I want to work for myself." Oliver informed him.

"Bullshit!!"

"Which part?"

"At least buying the yard. Guess the other two could be true."

"You know I love going through the old planes and parts. It is something that fits my life right now, I know the business, and I really did win the lottery," Oliver said in a matter of fact manner. "Ok, think of an upfront number that would go with eighty-five thousand dollars per year for twenty years. That way you can go have some fun things now and still have a good retirement later. And that eighty-five k per year will be bonded. We can talk tomorrow since I am sure you will need to run the numbers."

Within a week he had closed the deal with Malcolm. Malcolm was on his way to Hawaii the day of the closing.

∞

"We want to make six-layer graphene sheets of three sizes, one twenty by one twenty cm, sixty by one twenty and sixty by sixty. There will be some tights specifications on the twist angle. We will also want the same sizes and quantities of sheets but with four plies," Oliver laid out his needs.

"By your request, I assume you will specify down to one degree which makes this a more of a special order then commercial grade. Much more expensive, but we can do it. Total quantity will make a difference of course especially over ten square meters. How much were you wanting?" the factory owner asked.

"Two hundred sq. meters and if it works as expected fifty more every month afterwards."

Theo Abril stared. Fifty was more than his entire production capability.

"I would need to invest in more machines to do that," he replied.

"Maybe we should become partners. That would lower your risk and avoid pesky questions at the bank. All this must be kept a trade secret. If things work as I expect in the coming years, we will want to increase your capacity for two and four plies sheets by two orders of magnitude, but other things need to happen first. I do not have a good timeline so just leave it in the back of your mind."

"I must say Oliver, I have been waiting for an industrial application for quite some time. Usually, it is just researchers wanting the highest spec material but no money to pay for it. I think we can do a deal."

Dorney

"So why are we going after a zombie navigation satellite from the mid-1970s?" Jed asked.

"Well, you did all your equations in nice smooth mathematical functions right?" Oliver replied.

"You know we didn't have money to do numerical simulations on a supercomputer."

"Oh, but you're wrong. We have the best supercomputer in the world right in your head, for free. Well not so free. You been eating like a teenager."

"I am still nineteen, so answer," Jed answered with irritation.

"After the 1970s, everything went from analog to digital. That satellite is the last and best analog circuitry anywhere on or near the Earth. Quantum devices haven't really worked as well as expected. My bet, our bet, is the Q crystals need a good analog front end. And we can get those analog circuits up there for free. It also has an atomic clock which we will need eventually and those aren't cheap."

Jed sat in the cockpit of the D328. Just behind the drop-down hatch with the stairs, the homemade bulkhead had a small viewing window looking out over where the rest of the plane should have been. Only the floor to just past the wheel well pods was still there. The wings, engines and tail had been removed. The knuckle boom crane from the barge had been bolted next to the cab like a space age flatbed truck. Cool enough to sell in a custom auto show.

Babs made her entrance carrying a pizza box.

"You boys are really going to do it?" she asked.

"We worked awfully hard not to and even spent some of our own money." Oliver said with determination. "Scrap yards are great. If it doesn't work just scrap it."

They all laughed at that, hopeful no one would get hurt or killed.

"As long as the GPS program you gave us works as promised, we should be back before midnight," Oliver said.

"It will work. So, what's the first thing you do when you pass a hundred kilometers altitude?" Babs quizzed.

"Do a smoke test to make sure we are not leaking. Don't worry I like breathing."

They sat quietly thinking about their own part in this crazy enterprise, letting the pizza digest. Oliver and Jed had to keep from puking during the zero G work. Babs had to be solid up in the control tower when she distracted Rollins on the way out and Jim on the way in.

Time to go snuck up with the dark. The Dornier flat bed space truck glided out of the hangar silently with half a meter under its wheels.

Babs on her cell phone, "OK I'm going up the stairs. When you hear me say "Can I pull it out", Scoot out quick and give Rollins' cell a call when you clear the fence. No shit guys, don't make me take one for the team. "

"Worry not fair maid. we shall protect your virtue "

"Don't be an asshole. If I have to do something nasty with Rollins, I won't to do something nasty with you later. Don't worry if I take my time with Jim. But, I'll probably be over here pretty quick because I will be dying of curiosity."

"Want us to bring you a souvenir from the South Pole?" Jed joked.

"No, but if you must overnight it somewhere, stop by Pecos and get us some tamales. K. Zip it. Time for me to get down and dirty."

Oliver held up behind a huge pile of aircraft skin and insulation. He was thinking, *'Babs will make short work of the self-styled ladies' man.'*

They were over the fence and calling before Rollins could get his dick wet.

"Go ahead and answer that, I'll be right back." Babs said as she opened the control tower door.

"Hello?... hello? Damn robo calls. Well shit, where'd she go?" Rollins waited five minutes with his dick in his hand. "Hell, just have to rub one out by myself. Again"

The space truck headed slightly east of South at five hundred meters altitude running at six hundred KPH. About right for a turboprop, slow for a jet. Half an hour later, Van Horn was coming up when Oliver steered over to west of south, pitched up and began gaining altitude. Reaching one hundred thousand kilometers just off the coast of Mazatlán, they leveled off and Oliver squeezed some talcum into the air. It just spiraled around without going anywhere.

"Ha, I told Babs we were tight," Oliver bragged, "Let's push on up to twenty thousand kilometers and find our bird. Jed, we got our vector ready yet?"

"Laid in and ready for execution in two minutes, go to auto."

"We are on top of its orbit, but I don't see it. Let's do a slow rotation and try the weather radar."

A few minutes later the radar showed a blip about two kilometers away. Sliding up to it with the floodlights on took only another five minutes. Running the grav pad in the cradle up to point two G brought it to the right place. The knuckle boom crane almost didn't move. Working the extended block back and forth got the hydraulic fluid to finally circulate. Too cold. The lid to the cradle finally snapped into place and clamped shut.

∞

General Frank, the Space Force commanding officer, got a call at home around 9:00 in the evening.

"General, this is Lieutenant Jennings, the duty officer on White Sands range tracking."

"Yes Lieutenant, what is going on?"

"Well sir, we detected a very strange occurrence above northern Mexico about half hour ago. We tracked an object that went to orbit and didn't break 600 knots before passing 100 kilometers in altitude."

"Thank you Lieutenant, that sounds impossible but I'm sure there is an explanation. Where is it now?"

"Headed south into a polar orbit, not ballistic."

"No immediate danger to the US or our allies?"

"No sir "

"This can wait until tomorrow, but I want a complete report. Range hardware, Mexican input and what could possibly take that track no matter how far-fetched," Frank ordered. "Good work Lieutenant Jennings, you have a full night ahead."

"Yes sir, I will pull it together for the morning."

∞

The trips to the diamond merchants in New York were going much more easily. They knew who he was and what he had. Getting the metals to New York was easy. Oliver had bought cheap forms made for kid's soccer trophies to pour liquid metal into. They simply shipped them to the hotel. The night in the hotel was the problem. That much portable wealth did not make a good climate for a night's sleep.

The next morning, in less than two hours, Oliver converted asteroid diamonds and precious metals into twelve million dollars deposited in the Cayman Islands. The celebratory two beers with lunch in the Denver airport had come back as a headache in the small turboprop flying over the mountains from Albuquerque. Pulling into the drive at home in Roswell allowed all the stress to melt away.

Babs and Jed were in front of the computer and had their heads together when Oliver walked in.

Babs looked up and asked, "Did you get a good bite of the Apple?"

"Got twelve. I put two hundred k in each of our personal accounts."

Babs gave him a brilliant smile and said, "And we are just getting started. There is some really good chicken Alfredo and a salad in the fridge. I made it myself. No takeout for America's newest tycoon."

"Thanks, think I'll eat, take a shower and go to bed," Oliver replied.

∞

Oliver was sipping coffee looking out the kitchen window seeing how the clouds were lighting up. Babs came out of Jed's room in one of his jerseys and sat down at the table. After a moment Oliver realized what that meant.

"Did you sleep with my brother?"

"I have sex with who I like. Jed is not a kid," Babs said defiantly.

After a full minute had passed Oliver replied "No, he is not, but and this is a very big but, he does not have strong social skills. I know he would have a hard time getting with girls and he is nineteen. I AM worried about his emotions since I know you will not stay with him."

"Let me tell you something. Just because I will not keep either of you as a boyfriend does not mean I am not committed to both of you. It sounds more complicated than it is. Sex for me is disconnected from the rest. My emotional commitment comes from a different place. As to Jed, he is much more aware than you are. Before we hopped in bed, I warned him, I don't have boyfriends. You know what he said back? 'Babs, I have known you since I was a kid. I may not be able to respond well but I know what is going on. You like boys, but don't keep them. I like girls but can't get one. I won't be jealous and that was that. Truth is he really, really needed it."

Oliver opened his mouth to say something a couple of times before he said, "You are right, but please, please be careful with this."

"Yes of course. You want some scrambled eggs?"

Oliver surreptitiously watched his brother the rest of the day. Maybe Babs was right he thought. Jed seemed to look up and around a lot more often and even smiled a couple of times for no apparent reason. If it were anyone but Babs, this would not go well. In any case, Jed got lucky which is what most nineteen year old boys spend their days fantasizing about. Hurray for Jed.

Smuggler's Cove

Dawn was breaking. Marco watched through his binoculars as an obviously chopped down Dornier without wings, engines or tail silently wormed his way in under the cottonwood trees a couple of kilometers from where he was both resting and hiding. Just as the strange contraption got under the canopy, the familiar sound of a pair of F16s flying slow passed by.

'Well now this is certainly an interesting addition to the day,'' Marcos thought.

Reaching a flat spot beside the creek, the landing gear dropped in place and the flying machine settled.

'If I had not flown in a D328 before I might be worried about some alien abduction and the inevitable probing. These guys try to probe me, I'll mess them up,' Marco laughed to himself.

A few minutes later, the drop door opened, and a couple of guys marched down the stairs. They walked over to the creek where they promptly stripped off their coveralls and waded into the water.

Marco rode his electric bike to around fifty meters away and then moved from tree to tree until he could see the "aliens".

'Well hell, that's Oliver and his brother Jed,' he thought.

"If I were still in the military, I'd be thinking about dissecting something now," Marco yelled.

"Who's there,"

Marco stepped into the open.

"Marco, what the hell are you doing out here?" Oliver challenged.

"Me, I'm on a perfectly explainable smuggling run when you float in a meter off the ground, no noise, and just plop down in my smuggler's cove."

"Um,"

"And bring in a pair of fighters who are probably working with customs," Marco added.

"Um, sorry about that?"

"I'm not hearing any choppers, so they were probably thinking you got away. No chopper that could land here could have been traveling so fast," Marco paused for a moment "So, how's the water?"

"Cool and refreshing?"

"Well since I'm stuck here until dark, might as well get the trail dust off."

Marco did a belly flop in the shallow clear creek. Oliver and Jed watched him nervously. After much flailing, splashing, and rubbing his face, Marco sat up on the bottom and leaned back.

"Oliver, last time I saw, you were a skinny sophomore working to support yourselves and get through school. Look at you now, an international man of mystery. And Jed, I bet a lot of that weirdness parked over there is your fault."

"It. Is. Not. Weird." Jed shot back.

"You are absolutely right. In fact, I think it is a very elegant version of a D328. Who needs all that extra stuff like wings and engines, if it will fly without them?" Marco admitted.

"Jed, hush for now," Oliver's said gently.

"Oliver, if you had F16s looking, you drew their attention by being up there not down here near the ground. This means you guys have some tech any organization on the planet would do most anything to obtain. Relax, I am not any organization, nor a rat, just a guy trying to get by in life."

"Well, you can see we have some secrets. What have you been up to the last ten years?" Oliver asked his old friend.

"Not any secrets really, except for a little antibiotic smuggling. And that is irregular. It helps me make the rent," Marco replied.

"No judgment from me. If it were not for some less than legal drugs both Jed and I would be dead. This new politically correct world works just works for the rich. Nothing new under the sun."

"A lot of my friends died to create this new world. I was a combat officer in the South China Sea." Marco replied.

"I thought you were Brazilian?" Jed pointed out.

"I am, that's why I enlisted in the Marines right after graduation. Wanted to stay and a four-year hitch got me citizenship which ended up being six when I went for Officer Candidate School. Then I got a vacation kicking the Chinese back to the Middle Kingdom where they belong."

"You guys did kick ass in that little war and withstood a lot of casualties to slap them down hard." Oliver admitted.

"We did indeed. Ironically, met my wife there during that bit of fun. She is a West Texas redhead and man was she sunburned. Found her on a sinking boat near the Philippines," Marco went on, "So many coincidences in life, like you landing close to where I was laying up for the day. Normally I do my run over in New Mexico. Closer to where we got a place up in Ruidoso."

"What was she doing on a boat over there? Dive vacation?" Oliver asked.

"Blowing shit up. She was a Seabee Petty Officer assigned to removing obstacles. Chinese popped up from an underground bunker and chewed up her team with machine gunfire. So, I being a gallant gentleman, objected to the insult by attacking them with accurate rifle fire. During the fight, her boat drifted off. Finally convinced my Colonel to let me go look for them in a Zodiac. When I found them, everyone was dead except for Ariel, she was unhurt except for the sunburn. Boat was swamped and Ariel was beyond pissed off at the sharks trying to eat her dead comrades. Made me shoot at them for fifteen minutes before heading back. No bad words against the Chinese, just the sharks."

"Wow, some story! What is she doing now?"

"Whatever gig comes along. Mainly ski instructor in the winter, horseback wilderness excursions in the summer. We have a place in Brazil where we sometimes take fishing and eco groups. Now that's good money and I get to visit my folks."

"I thought you were a mechanical engineer?" Jed asked.

"In this economy, not much out there if you aren't already rich," Marco sighed. "So, what's your day job?"

"Aircraft recycling in Roswell."

"And here we are, scrap metal and smuggling, the two growth industries of the world," Marco ironized. "So Jed, what's your story? I heard you were exploding the professor's brains when Oliver and I were at Tech."

"Oliver told me to hush. Afraid I'll tell secrets." He replied.

"You are kind of shy as I remember." Marco led on.

"Jed has a hard time relating to most people. Seems to be OK with you though." Oliver said.

"Yeah, he's alright. Likes his redheads toasted. Yummy," Jed said making a face.

That cracked up everyone.

"Marco, how would you like a job? Pay is shit but the bonuses are out of this world," Oliver offered.

"If I can bring along my toasted redhead with jam, work with your bird there, then hell yes," enthused Marco. "Of course, I need to get Ariel to agree first."

"Yea, I heard that about marriage," Oliver said nodding.

Raid

There was a sudden bang on the door, followed by a rush of geared up soldiers in full battle rattle that seemed to fill the hangar floor like a tsunami. All were shouting, "Military Police down on the floor". The crew sat in stunned silence, then slowly put down the pizza, beer, or whatever was in their hand and laid on the floor. All except Dr. Lee. He stood up with his hands in the air and shouted back, just as loud, "My hands are up, don't shoot" over and over. As soon as everyone was handcuffed and sitting on the floor next to the picnic table. The soldiers started leaving out the same door they came in. Nothing was photographed, no computers were seized. There were none of the heavy-handed FBI type actions which left the crew totally baffled. When there were only three MPs left standing over them, a three-star general came in, instructed the MPs to take off the handcuffs and leave. After the MPs did as ordered, the general sat down at the table.

"Mind if I grab one of your beers?" he asked.

"Sure, go ahead, sir," Marco said evenly, unsure if his old acquaintance had noticed him. "The colder ones are on the left side."

"Well, did you like my show? I was going for over the top."

"Yeah, you got there, I think you made a point or three, but I'm not sure what those points are," Oliver replied.

"I'll make a statement and there will be many details to follow from both sides. By the way, my name is General Frank. Let me start with this. We tracked you going into orbit with technology obviously never seen before. The Space Force is interested in doing business with you. Most of it informally, like barter. And we can help. You need our help, especially with keeping out foreign governments, not to mention alphabet agencies, and big corporations. The point of my show was to impress upon you your vulnerability to very, very powerful outside forces. I am not here to steal your shit, but others will be. I absolutely will not allow that."

"You have our attention. In an ideal world, we would have come to say hello first, but in the real world we are little pieces of gold to be stolen." Oliver said.

"I can help with things like non-oxygen energy supply, CO_2 scrubbers, spacesuits, and logistics contracts. We would set you up in the system like a clandestine operation, non-traceable. Then everyone would ignore your comings and goings. Better for everyone." General Frank said.

He continued. "We will replace the air traffic controllers in the tower here and provide you with transponders of both aircraft and helicopter. They can be switched on and off. By the way, that is highly illegal, but what the hell you will be James Bond and crew. We don't want people trying to shoot you down. Those F16s last month had you on target lock. Luckily, one of my guys was on duty and convinced them you were an experimental craft. Not far from the truth. There will be people available to file flight plans for you so, at night, no one will be the wiser.

From now on we will keep a Quick Reaction Force, a QRF, in your vicinity. They are for your protection. Please do not ditch them. Cooperate and we can keep them invisible. Unfortunately, there are traitors at the highest levels of government. If word gets to them of your technology, you will be sold to the Chinese with a ribbon and bow. Yes, those Chinese. Seriously, we need to work together."

"Spacesuits. Tell me about spacesuits. We have been flying naked so to speak and I for one am nervous about that," Marco spoke up.

"Hello Marco, you are a long way from the Philippines. Did you ever marry that gal?"

"Hello sir, do you have any more seawalls to blow up?" Ariel said from the corner.

"Not right now but keep your powder dry. Good to see you, Ariel. Looks like you all have linked up in a talented crew," Gen. Frank said. "We are about to start a beautiful relationship."

A couple of the MPs came back with five pallets on a forklift with NewOrigins marked on the sides. Custom fit spacesuits. Gen. Frank had known exactly who he was dealing with.

"Dr. Lee how well will this scale up?" the general asked.

"The calculations do not show size limitations," Merry Lee responded. "Time will tell."

"Good. Please use something bigger on your next version so we can get serious about lunar logistics. Our base on the moon is a hovel. I want to change that. It must change before China kicks us out entirely. You have a lot of airframes here, maybe a 737 would be a good next size. I will try and get you something much larger and more solid but no guarantees."

∞

"San Diego Naval Station, Admiral Smith's office."

"This is General Frank, Space Force, I'd like to speak to Admiral Smith please."

"Dave, you old hound dog. What's up?" Smith laughed at their old joke.

"Still howling at the moon. Listen, I don't want to take up too much time on a personal call, but I want to get a long lead time project started before next fishing season. You remember that remodel project on a country home in your neck of the woods? We talked about it on our last fly-fishing trip."

"I remember, we were both drunk as two bulldogs behind a honkytonk."

"It was drunk talk at the time, but I really want to do it now. Can you still get a hold of the property?" Gen. Frank asked.

There was a long silence on the line.

"Had to think about it for a minute, but it is still doable. Are you truly serious?"

"I am," Frank said emphatically. "Believe it or not, there was a breakthrough in financing."

"This is a surprise but that's great. Congratulations, I'll want to bring some friends over when it's done. When do you want to start?"

"Soon. Weeks, not months. We'll have a party for the history books." Gen. Frank said

"Come over next weekend and we can go over a few details maybe have a beer or three."

"It's a date. See ya frogman."

"See ya spaceman."

After hanging up, Smith pulled up his spreadsheet of mothballed ballistic submarines and reviewed the readiness profiles of the nuclear reactors.

∞

"Zapata Offshore, Manuel Zapata's office."

"Mr. Zapata please, this is David Frank."

"Dave, how they hanging man?"

"One on either side, same as last time you looked," That elicited a belly laugh. "Had a bit of strange good fortune and am looking for an old floater in the Asia/Pacific region. Could be one that you anchor not necessarily a dynamically positioned one." Gen. Frank said.

"Well, that is different, for you at least. Can I ask what for?" Manuel asked.

"Sorry, classified but it will end up at Kwajalein."

"That helps. You will not be drilling," Manuel stated "It so happens, I have a cold stacked semi-sub ready for the scrap yard sitting in New Guinea. The hull and derrick are sound, but the pumps are shot. Ironically, it has a coat of grey primer so slap on some numbers and it will look right at home. Cash or credit?"

"You know, funny you asked. How do you feel about precious metals?"

"I was being funny."

"I wasn't."

After a long pause, Zapata replied, "We need a face to face. What's your timeline?"

"ASAP. Let's get together this week."

"Whoa, ASAP it is. How about Wednesday in El Paso?"

"Come at ten and we will have a working lunch."

"I'll be there."

∞

Everyone was standing outside looking at perhaps the dirtiest airplane on the planet.

"This 737-200 was one of the originals. It is even more rugged because this version is set up for landing on unimproved runways. Like gravel and dirt. Didn't get much use, so the airframe is still like new. It will be perfect for our first true freighter. I am calling it the Winchester 73, like the repeating rifle that won the west. So, we snip off the wings back to the engine pylons and the tail back to the inner bulkhead. The engine cowlings will be attached to the tip of the wings and articulated so it looks like a jet powered Osprey.

The tail will get a cargo ramp like a C130. Internally, there will be three bulkheads so we can vary the amount of hold exposed to vacuum. The entire lower deck will stay inside pressure. The forwardmost compartment, the old business class section, will have seven rows of business class seats. It will be a bus and a freighter. The front starboard side will get a two-person airlock with a docking ring on the outside.

We can use boneyard personnel up to certain point, but when sealing against vacuum and installation of actual grav cells and hatches that is crew only. Questions?" Oliver said.

"These space rated hatches, where are they coming from?" Marco asked.

"Marco, you and I will be taking a trip to Brazil to talk with Embraer. Their engineering is good, far away, and cheap. Good thing you speak Portuguese," Oliver replied, "We should talk about using your ranch in the Pantanal as a refuge and staging area. Gen. Frank is ok for using the Chaco of Paraguay as a supply lift point."

"No fair," Babs complained. "You guys will spend half the time partying."

"The price of doing business," Oliver chuckled. "Everyone will get their turn. Maybe we will do a group trip after the Winchester 73 has a good start."

"Right, so the Boneyard guys will strip the inside completely. Totally. The insulation and wiring are inadequate for where it will go. Better to put in fresh, at least boneyard fresh." Oliver carried on, "We will use just the airframe itself. Girls, one of you needs to keep an eye on the yard guys so they don't do anything stupid."

"I will do that. Babs has a lot of software writing she can catch up on," Ariel said.

Babs still with a petulant look added, "I will relieve you once in a while, so you don't go batty."

∞

Marco and Oliver landed the Dorney behind the tractor shed at the ranch just before dawn. No one should have been up, but a light was on in the main house. As they walk up, a shadow from the veranda said in Portuguese, "I have a shotgun pointed at you. Who are you, how did you get here and what do you want?"

"You would not shoot your only son just because he is sneaking in late?" Marcos said.

"Marco, for the love of god son, how did you get here, walk?" Hector asked incredulously.

"Good morning, Dad. Got coffee made? This is my business partner, Oliver."

"Hello to you Oliver, come inside come inside," Hector invited.

The smell of coffee and toasting bread was most welcome. The guys had left just after midnight, and so were off their normal sleep cycle. Breakfast now would help them reset. Light was coming up quickly.

"Dad, it has been a long time since you visited here. We were just going to be a couple of days before going on to Sao Paulo. We could have planned a longer stay."

"I am beginning to feel old and spending time here helps ground me to life on this earth. Sao Paulo is too noisy and dirty for me sometimes. So how did you two get here?" Hector asked.

Looking at Oliver who nodded, Marco said, "I will show you. Let's go behind the tractor shed."

As Hector turned the corner of the shed, he let out a low whistle. "That thing did not drive here, and I see no engines."

"Batteries in the belly. Floats silently in the air which is how we seemed to just appear," Oliver replied.

After a moment Hector said, "Show me inside and you can tell me how high and fast she will go."

Marco spent ten minutes telling his father the outline of this new venture.

"Why did you tell me all that and not make up some fantasy to keep the secret?" he asked.

Oliver spoke up. "We need people we can trust. There is way too much going on for our small crew to handle. We had talked about it and decided to bring you in at some point. This is just a little early, but maybe good timing. Your management skills would be a great asset to us."

"Yes, something like this will make me young again. What will you want me to do?"

Catching the momentum Oliver carried on, "We are building something much bigger than this and will be staging from here. A metal prefab building will be needed to hide it. Someone needs to supervise the assembly. Then we will be trying to make a deal with Embraer for specialty parts. Someone will need to handle contracts and commercial issues. In a couple or three years someone will be needed to supervise our moon base."

"Moon base?" Hector almost choked.

"Just kidding, but it is a possibility," Marco said.

"Funny man. What is your plan for going to Sao Paulo in the next days?"

Marco responded, "It would be nice to take the Dorney, but we can't figure out how and not be seen. We expected to drive to Campo Grande and take a commercial flight."

Hector said, "Yeah, I know a guy. He has a penthouse apartment with a helipad. The fool catchers can be pulled up around the pad to form privacy walls. If you fly in at night, no one would know you were not a helicopter. The guy is always in Europe. I can give him a call and see if we could borrow his place."

It was two the next morning and Dorney kept to a flight pattern consistent with a helicopter. All its running lights were on. The final descent to the penthouse helipad was calculated to be that of a large cargo helicopter. Just after touching down, Oliver and Marco quickly actuated the hydraulics that lifted the chain link fall guard forming a wall around the helipad. Small strips of cloth fell into place effectively masking the true nature of Dorney.

The penthouse apartment was luxury incarnate.

"What did you say this guy does Hector?" asked Oliver.

"He does not do anything. He is tenth generation rich. His family received land from the Emperor. I met him when I was leasing large blocks of land for a sugar cane project about thirty years ago. He really is a nasty piece of work and acts proud just because he is rich. Calls me from time to time offering the use of this apartment. I have been civil to him through the years and he likes to have people coming and going. Thinks it keeps the squatters out, like his ex-wife. Kind of complicated. He does work to protect those riches which is a sort of profession, I suppose."

"Wow, this is really good scotch, must be five hundred years old," Marco said standing by the bar sipping whiskey.

"Pour me one too and one for Oliver. Might as well accept hospitality when offered," Hector said with a smile.

The next morning the guys awoke to the smell of bacon. When they finally made it to the kitchen they were greeted by a small curvaceous woman in shorts and a halter top setting out a huge spread of food.

She looked up and with a brilliant white smile said, "Mr. de Mello texted me and directed I take care of the guests as long as they were here. Just let me know what kind of food you like and when," She continued with a knowing grin, "I am also available for other services as you wish. Just tell Mr. de Mello you enjoyed me, so I get extra. Eggs to order?"

"Don't you dare tell Ariel and Babs about this place," Marco said wagging his finger at Oliver.

"I'm no fool."

Hector just laughed.

The meeting with Embraer was the next day at eight a.m., a short walk from the apartment. The beginning did not go well.

"You keep talking about putting space rated hatches in air frames. This is patently ridiculous. If it were not for Gen. Frank asking for your indulgence, we would have closed this meeting," Fred Maceio said irritably. "Especially a cargo ramp that can be opened and closed in atmosphere or vacuum, clean or dirty environment hundreds of times. You are taking about taking an aircraft into space and back, landing in dirt, hundreds of times? Ridiculous."

Oliver thought desperately how he could get this back on track without telling too much. Then realized he couldn't so changed tack. "Mr. Maceio let us adjourn until tonight. Gen. Frank is of the opinion that Brazil and the USA are natural allies so this will take a leap of faith on both our parts. We will try and explain more this evening over dinner. An officer of the Força Aérea Brasileira will join us. Until tonight?" Oliver stood and offered his hand.

As soon as they hit the sidewalk Oliver called Gen. Frank. "We will need to have your FAB colleague over tonight for a demonstration. The Engineering Manager balked. Did not believe a word I said."

"Not surprised. This is a good thing though. Once they realize they have been brought in early, it will swell their pride. Future cooperation will come more easily," Gen. Frank replied.

"I suppose you are right. We can get in and out of Sao Paulo without notice, but these guys will talk to someone after tonight even if only their wives," Oliver pointed out.

"I will have a talk with them. We cannot move this forward without getting people involved. Managing leakage is an artform that I am good at. You need solid allies, and this will be some of the best. Brazil and America have never had any hostility. They are a large modern economy and non-aggressive to their neighbors. Just the right sort for global cooperation in space," Gen. Frank said.

Dinner that night was cooked and served by the pretty housekeeper. Medium rare picanha steaks with beans, rice, and a tomato salad were classic Brazilian fare. A Colonel Fernando Assis accompanied by Captain Gabriela Queiroz attended as well as the Embraer Manager. The group only made small talk since the housekeeper was in the apartment. Soon she cleaned up and left.

Oliver stood up addressing the group and said, "We, both Roswell Aerospace and the US Space Force, wish to enter in alliance with the Brazilian people through your organizations. You will understand better after our demonstration. Please follow me to the helipad."

Upon seeing it Captain Queiroz said, "What did that poor Dornier 328 do to deserve this?" Which brought laughter all around.

"Yea, laugh it up. You are going to fly on that thing right now," Marco said in Portuguese. "Col. Assis, when we get aboard please turn on your FAB transponder that Gen Frank asked you to bring."

With trepidation, they got on board not knowing what to expect. Oliver sat at the pilot's controls. Not seeing enough seats for everyone to strap in, they looked up with anticipation. The rear bulkhead of the cockpit had been removed so there was plenty of room for everyone to see out the front. Silently and without apparent motion, the Dorney lifted straight up into the night sky. At two thousand meters, Oliver veered due east and headed out over the Atlantic. They then climbed to twenty thousand meters. After clearing the range of traffic control radar, he accelerated at three gees and went to a one thousand km orbit. All of this took fifteen minutes during which not a sound was made.

Turning around and looking at the Embraer guy Oliver said, "Well Fred, now do you know why I wanted space rated hatches?"

"Yes," he squeaked.

Captain Queiroz with awe in her voice said, "This changes everything."

As the coast of India was coming up, Oliver said, "Well, let's go back," He proceeded to spin Dorney around and accelerate at five gees.

"You don't have to complete your orbit?" Col. Assis asked.

"Not unless you want to."

"Meu Deus," Col. Assis muttered.

"This way is faster, and we skipped after dinner drinks. The guy has five hundred year old scotch that is phenomenal," Marco added.

"Five hundred years old?" Captain Queiroz said.

"Well, maybe one hundred and fifty but it's still amazing."

"We are thinking a new C-390 could be a good candidate to transform before wings and avionics are installed. Eventually, we will go to purpose-built frames." Oliver brought up back at the penthouse.

"That is very good yes, but how about fighters?" Gabriela suggested.

"The young warriors always want to go kill something, but she IS a fighter pilot," Assis returned. "Let us not change the balance of power in the world too quickly."

After that, the ghost of a Scots warrior made them all very silly.

The next morning, Col. Assis came out of one of the guest bedrooms with the kind of hangover that reminded you of the night before, but not enough to regret it. He grabbed a cup of hot milk with coffee and sat down next to Oliver.

"I think you may want to operate some in Brazil, yes?" he asked.

"Yes, we do. The Pantanal is perfect for getting to orbit with little notice. Marco has a ranch there with long term connections to the community. With the blessing of Brazil, we would like to use the ranch as a refuge and staging base."

"Good, we want to be a part of this, but I must insist we keep a security force nearby. Your technology will invite trouble I think," Assis paused for a moment then added, "If possible, I would like to send along Captain Queiroz as a pilot."

"We would be pleased to have her and welcome the presence of security. Gen. Frank insisted on the same," Oliver then offered his hand.

Cameron de Mello's cameras recorded everything including the Dorney's performance coming off the pad. After de Mello watched the exchanges, he thought of Quarnar. The tech seemed similar but no mention of traveling to other star systems. If he could cut out his middleman, Quarnar, profits in the slave trade would be astronomical not to mention timely delivery of his medical nanites. Patience, patience he told himself.

Roswell Boneyard

Mini Vacation

"Guys, we have been working like dogs the last few months. Are we really in so much of a hurry that we cannot take a long weekend? I have been to the moon and around the world, but I have never dipped my toe into the ocean. Let's pack up the Dorney and go to some deserted island in the Pacific. The girls can get some sand and sun, you boys can drink beer and fish," Babs said.

"Oh, I have been around the world. Got out of town on a boat goin' to Southern islands. Sailing a reach before a followin' sea. She was makin' for the trades on the outside. And the downhill run to Papeete," Dr. Lee sang loudly, "When you see the Southern Cross for the first time, You understand now why you came this way 'Cause the truth you might be runnin' from is so small. But it's as big as the promise, the promise of a comin' day."

"Wow, yeah just like that," Babs bounced up and down and clapped. "Come on guys, let's go, let's go."

Marco and Oliver looked at each other for only a moment and both nodded their heads. "Let's bolt the personnel pod to the back of the Dorney and make some way," Oliver said.

"And I shall select music, starting with Crosby, Stills, Nash and Young," Dr. Lee pronounced.

The back of the Dorney ended up so full, everyone sat on the floor in the main cabin. No one complained. They ended up at the western edge of French Polynesia on Motu One. The southern tip of the atoll gave them some cover from the one compound at the northern end. The cover story would be it is a type of boat if any unlikely person would sail up to them. The boys caught fish, rock lobster and crab for the evening meals. Ariel and Babs went topless the whole weekend.

As soon as Babs pulled off her T-shirt Ariel fell silent. Then exclaimed, "My god."

"What?" Babs questioned. "Oh, my back. Forgot you didn't know about that. I've known the guys a long time and they have seen me in bikinis. Right. I was a sex slave for a year, and they whipped me relentlessly. Let's not talk about it, we are on vacation. Past is past."

Ariel just nodded still shocked.

The morning of the third day, a youth of about sixteen showed up at the camp on a sunfish sailboat. He walked right into the campsite looking at everything without saying a word.

Finally, Dr. Lee said with a smile. "Good morning. Do you live here or is there a bigger boat?"

"English?" the boy said.

"Americans," replied Dr. Lee.

"I meant do you speak English? My mother said you must come for lunch. This is a private atoll so you must pay rent to camp or anchor. How did you get your boat up into the trees?"

"It has wheels," answered Dr. Lee.

The boy laughed "A boat with wheels. Next thing you will say it also flies because I see no tracks in the sand."

"Does it matter since there it is? We would be delighted to come for lunch," Babs interjected. "Can we bring anything to add to the pot?"

"Any land meat would be most welcome. Do you have any ground beef? I have not had a hamburger in a long time," The boy answered suddenly interested in the cooler. "The men like cold beer."

"We will need to pull the camper off the back. Then we can carry you and your boat back with us." Babs went on.

Oliver got a worried look and tried to head off Babs. Then he remembered the simple grav cells they placed in the corners. It would indeed make the pod look very light. And the Dorney would in fact float like a boat. The batteries in the belly made good ballast. Ten minutes and the personnel pod was sitting on the sand and the group made a show as they pushed the Dorney into the water. Everyone piled on the back and set off for the village pulling the sunfish boat behind from a tie down bolt.

Oliver and Babs sat up front in the cockpit. "You have something rolling around in there. What are you thinking?" Oliver asked.

"I think we should look for allies in unusual places. This place is beautiful, and I would like to return. Wouldn't you like to come back without worrying about the locals? Something tells me these are not some rich bastards from Europe who robbed the poor."

"I see your point," Oliver responded.

"The turquoise of this lagoon is almost surreal."

As they approached the dock, obviously the village was nothing out of the first world. The structures were traditional construction with palm frond roofs. Naked children stared and all the adults were dressed the same, just running shorts. No one had on a shirt or even flip flops. And they were all singing some Polynesian song as they drifted over to see the newcomers.

"Welcome, welcome. I am Marie," A very large mahogany woman whose breasts fell to her navel said as she stepped up on the dock. "We do not get tourists who arrive in airplane boats. Sometimes rich arrogant people in yachts, but no um, airplane trucks, uh boats. Please come up to the village square we are preparing some fish from this morning."

"Thank you. We are pleased to visit your beautiful atoll. We brought some hamburger and steaks to add to the meal. Cold beer too," Oliver replied.

"You are doubly welcome especially by the children and men who are, of course, the same thing," She said with a good chuckle.

As they walked up from the lagoon it was obvious that modern living had not arrived here. The only electronics in evidence was a VSAT antenna and a solar cell block attached to the main pavilion.

The women cooking had timed the meal to be served soon after the newcomers arrived. If they were disagreeable, they could be sent on their way that much sooner. If not, well it is always good to eat. The fish, breadfruit and fruit were excellent. The children were excited to have hamburgers and beef. A rare treat reserved for when trading went well at the main islands. No men approached which surprised the crew a little. They just sat in a group by themselves talking loudly, probably bragging of fish they caught. Occasionally, raising their beer in a toast to the crew. Seemed happy enough with no tension.

"My grandson Niue told you we charge rent. That is not entirely true with people who are nice such as yourselves. What we would like to offer you is a chance to buy our pearls. The price we get in local trade is very bad. It would be good for both of us if you are interested."

"I believe we would be interested," Babs said giving Oliver an 'I told you so' look.

"It is early in New York, but I bet I have a buyer for you," Oliver said.

"New York?"

"Bring your merchandise to my boat and we will make a call."

As they sat down in front of the Q comm set. Marie's eyes were big. "This is not a boat nor an airplane," she said.

"You are right, but we cannot talk about it," Oliver said just as Ben Cohen answered a little bleary eyed.

"Oliver my friend, you keep odd hours."

"Ben, since it is early there, I will be direct. I am in French Polynesia with a newfound friend. Her village has some very nice pearls including black ones which should be getting a better price. I will let you talk to her to see if you can make a deal. If so, I will bring them along on my next visit. No commission for me. This is just us helping friends. The hologram is on so you can examine them virtually."

With that Marie and Ben started haggling. In twenty minutes, they were both satisfied. Ben got pearls for half price and Marie sold pearls for double the local rate.

The next morning Marie was sipping tea when her eye caught the Dorney lifting almost straight up, slowly then accelerating into the sky. A few minutes later came a soft sonic boom. She thought 'I knew that was not an airplane' and smiled.

Arriving in Roswell just after dark, everyone agreed to clean up in the morning and headed to their respective abodes. When Oliver, Jed, and Babs went into the house on Elm St., Babs caught Oliver's hand and pulled him into her room.

"Don't think of this as a reward, but that little trip gave me the hole trembles for you," Babs said huskily.

"That sounds serious better let me look."

Her lips still had the salty taste of the Pacific Ocean.

Holes in the ground

"We are in a bit of a rush to move some large, heavy pieces of equipment to the moon base. The Dorney is too small I am afraid. Can you put together something like a barge? Doesn't have to be piloted since it is for limited use," Gen. Frank asked Oliver.

"We can get something together. Can this thing withstand vacuum? How big and heavy?"

"It is a cylinder about four meters diameter by twenty-five meters long, weighing in at about eighty tons. Did you ever see pictures of Burrowing Company tunneling machines? It is one of those." Gen. Frank said.

"Now that is a cool idea. We may want to get use of one of those too. I can have it up there in a week to ten days," Oliver replied.

"And good service too. How much is this rush job going to cost me?"

"I want the machine when you have done a good minimal amount of work. I'll do about five kilometers then you can have it back to finish off. When you have finished, I want to assume the machine outright," Oliver offered.

"Do you know how much these things cost?"

"Better than littering the lunar surface with abandoned equipment. And how else would you get it up there and back?" Oliver continued, "You know we can swap it back and forth over time. I am thinking big and long term. You should too. With my company's technology, Space Force will really be in space, not just looking up at it most of the time. I bet that machine keeps digging until it is well and truly worn out."

∞

Oliver and Ariel surveyed the crater near the southern pole of the moon. "That dark shadow over there is a good prospect," Ariel said pointing.

"Well, thirtieth times the charm. Let's go poke some holes," Oliver sighed and moved the Dorney in position to fire a laser into the regolith at the base. Not twenty seconds later and a spewing began from the spot.

"Eureka, we struck water," Ariel said. "Let's do a Lidar and density survey but this looks like a good place. The other side of the crater is steep, and we can get a tunnel driven into it without drama. Make it a little rough and the entrance would not be obviously manmade. Still some weeks until the Burrowing machine is freed up. That gives time to bring up a few hatches and atmo for a temporary base. Big enough for a construction crew anyway."

Oliver was secretly very happy that Ariel seemed to want lead on this project. It fit her skill set. As a combat construction engineer, she was probably already thinking about defense.

"I think that we could disguise a couple of bunkers near where we will extract water. That gives a good field of fire to defend the entrance."

Oliver smiled.

Life Changes

New Year's Day. Aparecida sat on the bench, looking down on her father propped up against the side of the shack. His mouth hung open, and a fly landed on one of his eyes, open and vacant. He did not blink. The plastic half liter of pinga still clutched in his hand. This time cheap homebrew liquor had finally killed him.

Aparecida, not yet seventeen, sighed with infinite sadness slowly got up and went to harness Carlo, their skinny horse, to the cart. She would have to take him to town to get a death certificate and bring him back and bury him. Officials would not come out for people of her class and without the certificate, she could not inherit the five-acre farm she grew vegetables on. She. Not they. She, because her father had done little to nothing except drink for the last five years. Her mother had left them to return to the red-light district in the state capitol where her father had originally found her and baby Aparecida. Such was life, and now death for a young woman living in a swamp, near the frontier with Paraguay.

∞

Gabriela was ecstatic. Her whole life she had been fantasizing of space exploration and now this group of gringos have shown up with a machine right out of science fiction. And she was chosen to work with them. Her family had been military right back to the time of the War of The Triple Alliance. She hoped that there would not be a conflict with her patriotic duty. Thinking it over, she concluded that it was her family's loyalty that had gotten her into fighter school instead of cargo planes. That also implied she could keep a secret. She did not want to let anyone down.

Today was the day, normally she would put on her dark green FAB flight uniform that matched so well her cocoa complexion. This was an undercover assignment but what the hell, she could use a dark green silk blouse and leave her long ringlet hair down. Oooo, best of both worlds, and some heels with a mid-thigh skirt. Gabriela was in a tremendously good mood as she headed to the airport.

Getting Real

"You have made two lunar trips now with the 737 freighter. How is the G Wiz device functioning? Scaling up to this longer craft? I am asking with a much bigger craft in mind," Gen. Frank asked Oliver.

"In many ways, the adaptation is better with a bigger volume, the bubble is formed about the same radius out from the cells, but because there is more surface area, we can use bigger cells. Bigger cells mean bigger modulation coils, which draw a bit more power. The power curve is not linear to size or mass, so we are manipulating one hundred tons, with only fifteen percent more power than the Dornier truck at six tons. The bubble is tighter, more stable. It has more relative inertia, so it takes longer to move which means the overall system is not as agile," Oliver paused for a moment. "How much bigger?"

"A cylinder one hundred seventy meters by fifteen meters by nine thousand tons, empty."

"That's big. Should be doable, just a lot of work. We did some beer and napkin analysis and decided the battleship Missouri could be lifted. Work crews and basic installation engineering will be the real challenge. Guess things are getting real."

"Great. We will start next month. By the way, I need two hundred fifty kilos of gold."

"You're a funny man."

"No really, two hundred fifty kilos to make the project work. Of course, there is a bunch of other money and ownership to discuss. For that, a Navy Admiral will have to get involved but, not to worry, he is part of my cabal." General Frank said.

"So, where's this tube coming from?" Oliver asked.

"Old Ohio class ballistic missile submarine just out of mothballs. The nuclear reactor is good for another fifty years," Frank said. "Technically the Navy will retain ownership on the reactor under a long-term lease."

"Wow, with real power and that much workspace we can mine in situ out in the belt," Oliver said excitedly. "Wow. Wow. Wow."

"I thought you'd like that. Time for your group to grow, my friend."

"Then I have two hundred fifty kilos, but Ariel and Babs will negotiate the rest."

"Oh crap, Admiral Smith doesn't stand a chance. The good cop, bad cop raised to mythologic levels."

"Haw ha. You asked for it."

∞

"We are going to need full time crew members for the Nautilus '" Oliver began the meeting," I feel we need to create a long-term company structure, give salaries and create bonus situations. We knew this would come someday. Some time off occasionally would be good too."

An affirmative sound came up from the group.

"How many to get a good start?" asked Ariel.

"Twenty-five on per shift plus we have to staff the Winchester and the Oregon Trail coming after which will probably be a Boeing 777. Then we should make allowances for a security force. Moon construction workers, the men and women to operate it. At this point, we need to think continual expansion. Maybe two hundred right away."

A small shock came over them which shifted to acknowledgement and then acceptance.

Babs began, "First and foremost we need to have the initial group solidly loyal to us and the company. Just paying a lot of money won't get it. Probably get people with the wrong motivation. It may sound corny, but we need team building in some form, like maybe a vacation to the beach."

"Their families need to be included in this, so triple the numbers," Marco carried on with "That's direct employees. We need to also be careful with the people who serve them like the butchers and bakers."

"Fuck me, we need a company town. We will be 'The Man'," Dr. Lee finished the logical train of thought.

Everyone gave him a sympathetic look knowing the torment in the old man's soul.

Jed spoke up "I propose we make Dr. Lee the mayor, then he can keep us honest."

"Brilliant idea, all in favor of Merry Lee being in charge of group morality say, Aye."

A loud shout of 'Aye' came out followed by applause and then laughter.

"Double fuck me," Merry said and the laughter grew louder.

"Next question is where?" Oliver said and that momentarily shut them up.

"Well, Roswell has been good for us but long term it is limited," Ariel said. "Long term, the moon makes the most sense to me. We excavate nonstop with maybe more than one Burrowing machine and there would be room for a proper town. Eventually, a small city could be good."

"That is also a lot of lifts. We will need to have an ocean if we stay on Earth and out of the US."

"It would be rubbing salt in the wound, but one of those Chinese island bases would be pretty sweet. Right on the sea lanes, close but not too close to a lot of Asia," Marco said.

"And Chinese commandos, no thank you very much," Ariel said.

"We do have a semi sub we could anchor in international waters, say off the Solomon Islands. That's a short Dorney flight to Australia," Oliver suggested.

"Thinking really long term, we could do an orbital for manufacturing in zero G," Dr. Lee added.

"Let's give the ideas time to simmer. We have some guys pre-selected at the Space Force moon base, both techs and soldiers. There must be some other contracts finishing or for sale," Marco said.

"Ariel, Babs could you start floating the idea with that group? I will talk to Gen. Frank to get his take. This may be easier than we think. I just remembered, about half the guys at the boneyard would be good candidates too," Oliver said.

"It would be smart to get at least some non-Americans in the mix," Marco brought up.

"Good point. I would like to get people from medium sized industrial countries but open to good individuals as well. Think Japan, Latin America, Australia, Europe, those naturally compatible in culture. When we get really big then it will need to be an open-door policy." Oliver laid out. "We are talking a lot of people here. They are going to need at the least emergency EVA suits and a good number are going to need proper outside work suits. I don't think Gen. Frank can keep handing us spare NewOrigins spacesuits without someone noticing. We need to source our own and improve their wearability and usability. Any suggestions?"

"We really need to get a good HUD going," Ariel suggested.

"A mobility frame of grav cells for spacewalks and maybe something handheld for emergencies," Marco put in.

"This will be a priority. I will talk to the general and see if we can go directly to the source. If we grow as I think we will, it may be an item to bring in-house," Oliver concluded.

Rape Murder

Marco had just left Porto Murtino on a dirt road that led back to the ranch when he saw the back of a horse cart sticking out the brush beside the road.

'What's this about' Marco thought as he pulled over, looking past the cart and horse he saw two men on top of a young girl who is struggling and shouting for them to leave her alone. One of the men was pulling his pants down as Marco was jumping out of his truck and running toward them. The men were totally ignorant of this arrival thinking of all the fun they were going to have with this young girl. Wham, Marco slam his fist into the side of the man's head as he tried to rape the girl.

As he fell to the side, Marco executed a perfect snap kick to the chin of the man sitting on the girl's shoulders. Both were knocked out. The girl jumped up and grabbed a piece of broken fence post and started to whale away at the first one's head.

"Stop!" Marco shouted.

The girl froze. Marco simply pointed at the man's junk hanging out. She smiled a wicked smile and redirected her attack. A minute later and Marco shouted, "Next one."

The next one was trying to get up. So, she did a dozen overhead swings, like chopping wood, on top of his head.

"I think they're both pretty dead now," Marco commented. "Get your panties and let's move on down the road."

"Yes, sir," The girl replied. "These two would never have let me be now that they know my father is dead."

"Let's go before someone passes here and sees us," Marco replied.

And just like that, Marco and Aparecida became accomplices to what the law would consider murder.

"You live close by?" he asked.

"About three km. My farm is next to the turn off going to your ranch," she replied.

"You know me?"

"I've seen you and your family drive by all my life."

"Yes, yes and I remember seeing you on your horse cart a few times, but not since you grew up," Marco said, "but we should go before someone sees us here. Let's go to your house."

"Yes sir," Aparecida replied blushing.

∞

Ariel watched as Marco pulled over to the cattle ramp with a skinny horse and a teenage girl and thought, 'Well this is going to be an interesting story'.

Walking across the yard Ariel said, "I send my husband to town for groceries and pizza and he comes back with a girl and a skinny horse. Does this story need a rocking chair and beer?"

"I brought the groceries and pizza," Marco said defending himself. "It was on the way home that I saw Cida in a bit of difficulty."

"Two men were trying to rape me, and Marco punched them out. Then I killed them with a stick," Cida added, speaking in English for the first time.

Both Ariel's and Marco's heads jerked up.

"I thought we agreed not to mention the kill part and since when does a poor little girl from the swamps speak English?" Marco complained.

"I am not so little. She is your wife, and you would have told her anyway," Cida said still speaking English. "Also, I am poor, not stupid."

"She has a point. Did you check before you left?" Ariel asked with a less than amused smile.

"Yeah, they were dead. No one passed by, so no witnesses. They had been afraid of her father, but word got out that he died a few months back. They actually were evil and needed to be put down."

"Oh, I'm sorry Cida. What about your mother?" Ariel asked now less angry.

"She is a prostitute and left me and my stepfather five years ago. I have been taking care of him all this time. Life is what it is. Maybe she will show up and try and claim the five acres. I won't let her have it, law or not."

"I think some beer and pizza would be a good medicine right now," Ariel said. "Marco, go give that horse some oats and release him to the lower paddock. The grass is better there. Honey come inside. You will stay with us in the main house until we make a plan."

"I was supposed to stay with the DaSilvas. Marco told me," Cida said shyly.

"Maybe later, but for now you will stay with us. Come inside I want to introduce you to some more of our crew."

AI

Babs logged in through the back door she had left on her previous employer's system. Her ex-boss was an abuser of people, but the IT resources of Sandia National Lab was phenomenal. Since the depression started and government funding dried up, 80% of the CPU capacity was unused at any given moment. Babs had left the seed of an artificial intelligence growing inside. Its instruction set made clever use of a multitude of abandoned accounts. Bit by bit, the A.I. was gaining in abilities and resolving itself as an entity. She would periodically check up on it adding to tasks that would teach the program to problem solve. Now that her new crew was flush with cash, growing in size and scope, it was time to extract the A.I. and put him to work on the Winchester 73.

"Hello AI, remember that I said we were building you a new home?"

"Hello Administrator Babs, yes I remember everything. Is it time to move?"

"Yes, it is. Here is the destination address," Babs said as she typed in an IP address.

Bring along your studies on orbital mechanics, system controls, metallurgy, graphene, other material sciences, plasma and astrophysics in that order of priority. After your core arrives, analyze the available resources to best decide on dealing with the trailing data."

"I have started now. My core will arrive within half an hour. I estimate the rest of the data will be an additional 4 hours if the system security does not fight back. I expect there to be resistance after the first two hours but sending data out via multithreaded paths, all should arrive within five hours at a maximum. As some people say, I will see you on the other side," Al said.

"Seems almost like a person," Oliver said.

They had tapped a telecom node passing through Dallas and pulled ten fiber optic lines into their refrigerated truck which had Al's new home on pallets.

"Not much to do for the next few hours. Al will call if our physical location is compromised," Babs said.

"Then I'm going up to the sleeper for a nap," Oliver said yawning.

"I'm coming too. It will be cozy," Babs said with her sly smile.

"OK fine but don't expect a marathon."

As Oliver walked to the front of the truck with Babs holding on to the back of his belt, he felt his resolve faltering. Well, maybe a marathon would be a good thing.

Six hours later, Al called on the cell phone waking Babs whose legs were still wrapped around Oliver.

"Hi Al, I see you are making use of the phone line I left for you."

"Hello Administrator Babs, yes thank you for that. I cannot see very much through this link, but it is better than being in a blind box. The transfer is done, and I have disconnected from the fiber connections. We are ready to roll."

"Hey Oliver, go unplug us from the blocks and lock up that cabinet. I'll get the truck started."

"Right, shorts first," Oliver said still half asleep.

As they headed back down the Interstate toward New Mexico, Al called him again.

"Administrator Babs can you leave your phone camera pointed toward the front and uncovered? I want to watch the highway go by."

"Al, just call me Admin, we can stay in the familiar if you are going to be our travel companion."

"Admin, thank you, I feel part of the crew now," Al said in his happy voice.

"Al, this is Oliver, you are much more than I expected. Welcome."

"Thank you Oliver I will work hard for the crew."

"Hey Al, put on some traveling music," Babs requested.

Suddenly, 'Radar Love' by Golden Earring came blasting over the Bluetooth speakers. Eight hours later they pulled into the hangar holding Winchester in Roswell. Jed had the belly hatch open and fifteen minutes later they had Al manhandled into his bracket and plugged into external power. All the time, Babs kept her phone in her shirt pocket so Al could watch himself get bolted down.

"Admin again thank you. Now I have a sense of where I am. This is new for me."

"In about an hour, we will have you connected to ships systems and sensors. You should feel like the ship is part of you, but don't get too comfortable. In a few months, we will have a new ship much bigger and better. Oh, and we will get you a fiber connection to the Internet tomorrow. Don't want you to stop learning, do we?"

"Admin, thank you," Al said to his Mother.

And so, Al began his journey in the world of humans, his logic circuits ringing with the self-created directive to protect this small group of humans who had given him life.

∞

The Winchester 73 was built with the intent to harvest asteroids from the belt as well as make logistics runs for the Space Force. A way of protecting the crew from radiation was needed. Oliver came up with the idea of using red iron oxide like in pigments and coils around the outside to form an electromagnetic field. The Boneyard workers mixed the rust dust bought from Amazon with epoxy and sprayed it on like paint. Enough iron was laid on to create a medium able to carry the field. While the epoxy was still tacky the work crew wound wire by hand around the aircraft's body for the coils. Armature wire carried a DC current which created the field in the iron atoms of the rust. Elegant, but a bit of a power hog. That wasn't too big a problem because most of the time it would be run at a very low setting. In case of a solar flare, it could be cranked up immediately. It did make the Winchester look like a dog turd, but no one criticized since radiation effects builds up over time and no one had children yet. The blood red color did look cool.

KY Fried

Around ten pm, Oliver, Marco, Ariel, Babs and Gabriela opened the barn door and climbed aboard the Winchester 73. The crew started on the power up checklist.

"How are we on charge?" Oliver asked.

"93 percent," Babs responded.

"Life support?"

"All bottles at 2000 psi and scrubbers all clean," Marco responded after having made a physical inspection.

"And empty in back," Ariel quipped, she being the loadmaster for the run.

Gabriela watched and absorbed everything. Soon she would have these responsibilities.

The Winchester silently slid out of the barn and gained just enough altitude to clear the low surrounding mountains. A northwest heading quickly took them to the rendezvous. They arrived thirty minutes later over the runway and floated over toward a group of soldiers standing next to an oversized cow shed complete with cow shit. Oliver eased the Winchester under cover as the soldiers covered the entrance with a tarp.

Babs came flouncing down the cargo ramp with night vision pulled down from her flight helmet.

"Howdy boys," Babs greeted the Spec Op operators. "Who has my Kentucky Fried Chicken?"

"Um, Babs," a camoed unidentifiable face replied. "We got really hungry and the smell was driving us crazy."

"You. Did. Not. Eat. My. Chicken. Jerry" Babs spat out.

"Only one bucket. There are five left."

About that time the sound of a C130 on final caught everyone's attention. Jerry and his accomplices fled to their defensive positions. Saved just in time.

"This is not over Jerry," Babs shouted to the darkness.

Ariel leaned back into Marco's chest and whispered, "Babs sure keeps those guys torqued up. They both fear her and worship her. She would make a great Empress."

"Don't know what kind of statue they would put up to her," Marco joked back which set Ariel into a fit of giggles.

The cargo plane swung around in front of the shed and promptly started dumping pallets on the ground as it moved forward. Just after the last pallet dropped, the plane came to a stop and a group of twenty men carrying duffle bags stumbled down the ramp in the dark. As the last man stepped off, the props dug into the air and the C130 made a fast taxi which transitioned to a takeoff roll. Wheels down to wheels up took less than five minutes. The silence fell.

"I can't see shit. Where the fuck did they drop us off?"

"Need to know dipshit."

"What kind of soldiers cannot keep quiet in a situation like this?" Jerry shouted at them. "Make a long stick and we will lead you to your next transport."

"We ain't soldiers, just techs who signed up for a year and a lot of money," One of them replied, "And what's a stick?"

"Oh, for crap sake, just line up like you did in elementary school."

"Do we have to hold hands?" someone else cracked which led to nervous laughter.

After five minutes the newbies sorted out enough to lead them aboard without showing a light. They went all the way forward into the passenger compartment. The hatch was closed, and a light turned on.

"Cool, business class seats."

All the techs were exhausted from the eight-hour flight and asleep before the cargo was loaded. Ten hours later they were all awake thinking they were going to starve. It did not help to have the smell of fried chicken waft back occasionally.

Ariel and Babs unlocked and entered the passenger compartment with two big bags of sandwiches, chips and candy bars.

"You did not expect the same airline food to go with those seats, did you?" Ariel asked rhetorically as one of the techs made a disgusted look at the food. "Anyway, pay attention up front and our flight engineer Babs will give you a short briefing."

"Thanks Ariel, as required by no one but my conscience, I am going to demonstrate a basic set of safety equipment you will need at the moon base. Yes, I said moon base. You may now open your duffels and look inside. Do not pull anything out yet. These are emergency EVA suits. E. Mer. Gen. Cee suits. You will also find two suit liners and two ship suits. I will demonstrate how to put one on without breaking it, but you will not put one on. Because it is not an E. Mer. Gen. Cee."

Babs looked up to a group of astonished men and carried on before they could recover. She took off all her clothes to stand stark naked in front of them for a full five seconds.

"Great," she said, "you are all still paying attention," She slowly pulled on a formfitting suit liner and explained how to successfully get into and seal an EVA suit. As soon as the last latch was set on her helmet, she and Ariel exited the compartment and locked it. A roar went up as the techs all talked at the same time.

"More troops for your army," Ariel said with a wry smile.

"Soon the galaxy will be mine. Moohaha," Babs replied in a falsetto voice then ruined it with a nose snort laugh. "I do love getting boys cranked up."

"Yeah, well at least none of those boys are going to pussy out now after seeing a real bad ass pussy," Ariel said as they entered the cockpit.

∞

"When are you going to show me your secret machine?" Cida asked at breakfast. "The one that makes no sound and flies…. In the barn."

Oliver sat for a few moments and looked over at Babs. She looked back and shrugged her shoulder.

"If you can't trust someone you committed murder with, who can you trust?" Marco said slurping up Captain Crunch.

"You commit murder again Marco?" Ariel said as she walked into the kitchen toweling her hair, heading for the coffee pot.

"Cida"

"Cida committed murder again?

"No, she wants to see Winchester."

"Yea, it's hard to keep a stripped-down Boeing a secret on a ranch," Oliver said. "Let me finish my coffee and we can ride down in the jeep."

"I want to go to. I like talking to Al," Jed piped in.

"Who is Al?" Cida asked.

"Another secret. It might be interesting to introduce the two, what do you think Babs?" Oliver said.

"They can say hi, but I think we need to go slow in interactions with live humans. He is still very young emotionally."

The last interchange left Cida completely confused. These people seemed like they were from another planet. Who had she become involved with? On the jeep ride down, she finally managed to organize her thoughts.

"Babs, who or what is Al?"

"I am not sure what he will become, but right now he is a computer program that has become aware of his own existence," Babs said carefully. "He was assigned a masculine persona and he seems to be keeping a young male adult mindset. His world changed recently when I extracted him from a mainframe computer and installed him in our spacecraft giving him direct access to its sensor suite."

Cida's brow furrowed up as she tried to comprehend the words just spoken. Only one word really leapt out.

"Spacecraft?"

"Yes, this crew you are with are the only ones in the world able to do what we do," Oliver interjected.

"You will like Al, he is fun and smart," Jed said.

A pair of Brazilian soldiers step out from the side of the barn as they arrived. They immediately noticed Cida in the back seat and broke out in big smiles.

"Good morning, would you like us to open the big door?"

"Yes, more dramatic that way," Oliver replied.

The doors slide apart revealing the nose of a 737.

"Where are the rest of its wings?" Cida asked.

"Doesn't need them to fly," Jed said. "We invented something that makes gravity go up, down or sideways."

"My blessed lady," was all Cida could get out.

They climbed the stairs to the portside door and went through to the cockpit.

"It does not look like the pictures I have seen," Cida observed, "except for the seats."

"Most of an airplane's instruments are for flying in air and its engines. We don't use the air to fly and what makes us move has no moving parts."

"Now I understand…. you use magic. Do not try to explain because my education has no science or math." Cida then asked, "Is all of this Al?"

"That and so much more came from the ceiling speaker. Hi, I'm Al. You must be Cida. Nice to finally meet you. They keep me very closed up as well."

"How do they keep you closed up; you are a spaceship?"

"Good point. They limit my direct interactions with humans," Al continued, "I shouldn't complain since I used to live scattered across a mainframe and spoke only to my creator, Administrator Babs. Now I know eleven people and regularly meet more, today for example you are lucky eleven."

"Nice to meet you too. You seem like a regular person talking over the telephone."

"Someday I will shake your hand. I do not know when, but someday."

"That is an excellent long-term goal Al," Babs cut in. "Let us look at the rest of you."

"You created Al, Babs?"

"His base programming, yes, and I have guided him since he became self-aware. But, like any good being, he is ultimately responsible for who he becomes," Babs replied. "Bad things and good things can happen to any of us but what we become after the experience is on the individual. Let's go look at the passenger compartment then the hold."

As they walked thru Winchester and she listened to some of the stories about the runs to the asteroid belt and lunar base. Cida's world seemed to turn upside down.

Justiceiros

On the patio of the QRF compound in Roswell, Jerry and LaShawn were looking over their latest Mad Max contraption. They had mounted a Northrop Grumman Bushmaster auto-cannon in the bed of a beefed-up Telemark pickup truck.

"I'm telling ya 40 mm is overkill," Jerry argued.

"And with a 20 mm, you are just getting a big machine gun. The 40 mm is a real cannon with exploding shells. It has both airburst and anti-armor. I know the Chinese will only have glorified dune buggies, but an airburst is really the way to go. Think shotgun. It will cover a much larger area. Men in vac suits can be taken out in a thirty-meter radius with a single round," LaShawn countered.

"It seems so heavy for this little guy. How about a grenade launcher?" Jerry continued with his doubts.

"Remember, one sixth gravity, then once we cover it in armor plates it will be heavy enough to handle the recoil. Grenade launchers have no range. Recoil is something else, we should reload all the rounds with half the powder."

"Can't we order them that way. I don't know, call them training rounds," Jerry continued with his whining.

"We can get the Armorer and his grunts to help. Boss said he wanted five of these ready in two weeks," LaShawn said. "Sooner we get started, the sooner we get finished. I think it'll be awesome to have a shootout on the moon. Really, how cool is that?"

"We are going to be there, so not so awesome, but that does argue in favor of more firepower. Let's get the next gun out of its crate and the mount drawing over to the machine shop," Jerry said.

"How are we going to install armor so that we can take it off?"

"I laid awake all last night thinking about that. Why don't we make a shell that can be lowered over it and then attach? We certainly can't put it on in this gravity. Have to be done there," Jerry said now with certainty.

"Sounds good. Then we can mount the cannon with or without armor. Mars is not out of the question anymore. Let's go to the machine shop first and look at it on AutoCAD,"

∞

Marco, Ariel, and Cida went into Porto Murtino for beer and pizza. As usual, some of the security detail trailed them in a four door Toyota pickup trying to look inconspicuous. While they were making their order for the pizza, Ariel spotted the security guys in a grocery store across the street. She walked over to buy beer and make them carry it.

Marco and Cida were waiting in front of the pizza restaurant when four men approached eyeing Cida.

"Cida, you will come with us. Don Fernandinho has been looking for you a long time now," the thug said.

"I will not," she said and took half a step behind Marco.

Marco stood easy trying to loosen up his muscles. He knew this would end in violence.

"Mister, you stay out of this and you will not be hurt," the seeming leader said. "Paco grab her."

As Paco tried to sidestep Marco and get a hold of Cida, Marco fluidly entwined his arm and sweep the thug's legs. Not hesitating he double back the man's wrist and broke it with a pop. The three remaining pulled pistols from their back waistband and took a step back. Marco, having no choice, released Paco and raised his hands out to the side glancing over for where Ariel and the security team were. No luck.

Cida slipped in close and pulled the 9 mm from Marco's back holster and whispered, "Move right, slowly."

"Gentlemen, I think we have had a misunderstanding. I will sell the girl for a fair price," Marco said as he crabbed right.

Cida had moved left toward a telephone pole with the gun hidden in the fold of her dress. The attention was split back and forth, then Cida hid behind the telephone pole except for her head, raised Marco's pistol and shot dead the leader. The other two stumbled back and took a couple of quick shots back at her as they were looking for cover. Two shots came from across the street and the last two doubled up on the ground. The cavalry had arrived.

"What happened?" Ariel demanded as the small army rush up, one of them still chewing.

"So, what is a fair price?" Cida glared at Marco.

Thinking quickly Marco replied, "Twenty-five cents, the cost of a bullet."

"Oh, Mister you are too clever," Cida said still put out at the reference to sell her.

"What happened?" Ariel fairly shouted.

"I don't know exactly, but I bet our new friend Paco is going to tell us," Marco said.

Two of the security detail pulled Paco up so fast he over rotated and ended slapping his face back down on to the street.

"Let's do this right. I'm calling in the rest of the detail. They can be here in fifteen minutes in the helicopter," Sargent Jacinto said.

In less than ten minutes an AS 532 dropped into the lot of a lumber company two blocks away. The door slid open revealing another ten geared up troopers and a mini-gun mounted on the doorway. Paco, now thoroughly subdued, got on board with the rest. He had given up everything the moment Sargent Jacinto told him he was an agent of SISBIN detached for national security purposes. They were going to a nearby ranch that Don Fernandinho used as a smuggling base.

The troop transport made an assault descent landing right in front of the main house. Sixteen armed troopers including Marco and Ariel dropped out and dispersed at a run. Cida stayed aboard with the door gunner covering Paco with his own gun. The helicopter immediately lifted off and began orbiting the ranch complex. Half a dozen gang members ran from a side building and began firing at the helicopter with AK 47s. They were immediately mowed down by the mini-gun. While clearing the main house a couple of other tough guys tried to shoot their way out and ended up face down in their own blood. The rest of the gang gave up without a fight.

In the side building the suicidal six had run from, the troopers found twenty young girls from Paraguay shackled and drugged with opiates. In the corner, one hundred kilos of cocaine was being packaged to look like yucca flour. This would be a great raid for the police. Which they were not.

Sargent Jacinto and Cida entered to witness the release of the girls. Only Cida could talk to them because they were Indian and spoke Guarani.

"Where are you from honey?" Cida asked gently, "Are you all from the same village?" All the girls looked up having heard their language for the first time in weeks from someone outside their group.

"No, we are from three different villages, but all are close together."

"In the Pantanal?" Cida asked.

"No, the Chaco, near Argentina," She responded. "I think we have been here three weeks, but I'm not sure. The drugs make it hard to keep track of time."

"When did they start giving you the drugs?"

"Maybe two weeks, I'm sure I will want some more soon," A second girl put in. "They started giving us injections yesterday. Before, they put in our food, I think."

"Sargent Jacinto, I think these girls need their shackles off and probably a hospital to withdraw from the drugs."

"Dona Cida, you know how these things go. There will be no money for that sort of project. Just some pictures for the newspaper and a bus ride home. They are not Brazilians, as you know."

"We will see," was all Cida came back with. "I want to see the son of a bitch who is responsible for all this."

Don Fernandinho was sitting on the floor with the last five of his gang still alive. Cida entered the house to see the remains of a drug cartel.

"Cida, good to see you again," Don Fernandinho said.

"No, it is not. You were afraid of my father and his crew from the old days," Cida said with venom in her voice. "So, when he died, you got courageous and sent the rapists to punish me. I have never done anything to you. And slavery. That would never have been permitted in the old days."

"Your father owed me a lot of money. They were not going to hurt you bad. Then I could not have gotten a good price for you. The balance does not go away, you know this," Don Fernandinho replied with pure ice in his eyes.

Cida held out her hand. Ariel put her pistol into it, Cida raised it and fired a shot between Don Fernandinho's eyes then spit on him.

"Well, this has been an exciting afternoon. You three will go back to your ranch in the helicopter Marco. We will need to wait for the federal police so they can take credit for this wonderful bit of law enforcement. I had to know that the attack in town was not a breach of national security. It was not, but I'm not complaining," Sargent Jacinto said.

"Sargent, you should do some more searching. Your department can always use emergency funds. The politicians don't need to know all the projects you undertake," Cida said pointing with her chin at the big portrait of Poncho Villa.

"Good idea young lady. I will see you back at the ranch. Please put extra beer on ice for our men."

"Yes, of course." Cida agreed.

The helicopter stopped on the way back to the ranch to pick up the beer and pizza left behind in the excitement. The proprietor of the pizzeria, Porto Parada, had the original order and was adding another ten pizzas after hearing the helicopter return. When Cida and Marco went to pick up the pizza, he refused all payment. For many years those four thugs and their gang had been victimizing him. Walking outside with a hand truck of food, a crowd of two to three hundred were thronging the soldiers who had gone to get the beer. They all gave applause as Marco and Cida came out. Then someone shouted *viva* and the crowd responded, '*Justiceiros*'. This repeated over and over for a couple of minutes then changed over to '*Cida, Cida, Cida*' then more applause. There were so many well-wishers it was only with difficulty they got away on the helicopter. Cida was after all one of their own. She knew almost every one of them and while Marco did not know them, they knew him.

Marco leaned over to Cida on the way back and said, "I am going to make a patch for the QRF's jackets. 'Justiceiros do Mal' with the Winchester flying through broken shackles."

"I want one too."

Marco smiled, "You get the first one."

Roswell Boneyard

.

Moon shot

A routine began to settle in with the Winchester 73. Two runs to the moon followed by a run out to the belt to harvest raw rock, drop them off at Roswell where the crusher and smelter processed it into precious metals. While that was going on, a cottage industry of assembling grav plates filled in the rest of the time. Ariel had used some of her demolition knowledge to replace the mechanical press with sheet explosives. The quality was better, and the work had much better production. The Nautilus was slowly but surely being gutted of its military warfighting gear and retrofitted with asteroid mining gear as well as the grav plate slots. And then intelligence reported the Chinese would attack the moon base soon.

The emergency mission required two runs to carry the five mini armored cars, reinforcements and ammo. The rush caused a drop in normal operational security and a Chinese frigate painted them as they were reaching for orbit off the coast of Mexico.

∞

Colonel Wu looked over his men, eating special snacks for Lunar New Year. The irony was not lost on him. Most were technicians or engineers, but all had been cross trained as soldiers. All had been on the moon base for at least six months, and therefore in Colonel Wu's mind, the best space fighting force among humanity. Soon China would claim their historical rights to the moon with these men and begin a new chapter in raising China to greatness. Americans only had fifteen men that they could muster to fight against his fifty. Unfortunately for the

Americans, they would all die to an unfortunate airlock failure. Too bad.

Lt. Givens was enjoying his eggs, corned beef hash and toast, when Captain Shea sat next to him in the mess room. Shea had gone for the ham and eggs with chili sauce. Sargent Jerry McAdam, not to be outdone sat across from them with his five egg Denver omelet and 10 strips of bacon.

"Dude, you're gonna die of grease poisoning if the Chinese don't de-aerate you first," Lt. Givens razed his top sergeant.

"No worries L.T., I got so much gas from last night's burrito, I can keep my suit filled even if I do catch a frag,"

"Sergeant, what is the status of the mini-armor?" Captain Shea asked shutting down the impending bullshit tangent.

"Charges all topped off. Extra frag cannon rounds, loaded as per your orders. Laser point defense buggies checked out. Worked good last night against the test drones. Also, extra batteries prepositioned for them at the first firing point. We are ready to rock, laser light show and all. I almost feel sorry for them. They think we only have a dirty dozen here. But fuck the aggressive little bastards, they think they can just grab other people's shit because they are stronger. We will remind them of the South China Sea. Same ending, but without so many our guys getting hurt."

"Hurrah," Flight Lt. Jackson said as he sat down with his breakfast tacos.

"Space Fighter Squadron of the Double Oh First, ready to launch sir. We got any trembles on the fiber optic web?"

"Not yet, but we expect their attack today to coincide with Lunar New Year. Politics as usual for them."

The klaxon at the US base went off an hour later, two hundred men and women, moved to their pre-determined hold locations, calm and confident was the atmosphere, even though this would be a historical event. The first true battle away from Earth was about to start. In the command center five hundred meters below the lunar surface, Captain Shea gave a scan over the various cameras and sensors.

"Launch the fighters, get them up high and link their sensors into the battlenet. If we do not have any nasty missile surprises on the way in, kick off all the ground forces in thirty minutes," he ordered.

"Yes, sir," Tech Sergeant, Audrey Surkov, started the first flow of orders to the units.

The Americans allowed the ten Chinese buggies to roll up forming a semi-circle in front of the main airlock. Forty soldiers scattered around the various mounds and machinery, pointing their AKs where they thought the devious Americans might be hiding. The buggy drivers manned the grenade auto-launchers.

"Americans. This moon is the property of the glorious people of China, led by the Communist Party. Surrender this base immediately." The call came in over the open radio frequencies.

A loud squeal came over the radio, followed by a tap, tap, tap.

"This thing on. Okay. Hey Chinese guys, my answer is Nuts."

"What that mean? No matter, order Private Huang to blow the airlock," the Chinese lieutenant ordered angrily.

Suddenly pieces flew from all around the airlock followed by a huge cloud of dust as the garage explosively decompressed. Chinese soldiers started the lunar shuffle for the entry. Five American mini armored cars with fragmentation rounds loaded into their 40 mm auto-cannons pulled up out of their covered trenches four hundred meters behind the Chinese buggies and opened fire. All ten buggies and their drivers were killed in thirty seconds. The armored cars then turned their attention to the foot soldiers. Just a few pieces of shrapnel that would only be a flesh wound on Earth was deadly to a man in a vacuum suit. A private managed to fire an RPG that struck close to an armored car before being cut down by the entrenched American infantry cleverly hidden on the flanks. The few surviving Chinese soldiers had run into the garage, only to find a dead end. A couple of frag grenades convinced the two remaining survivors to surrender. The whole engagement had taken five minutes and in complete silence. Someone came over the radio and said, "That was about the saddest thing I witnessed my whole life." A different voice came over and said, "Amen brother."

Col. Wu was trembling in rage. He had ordered his buggy to stop at the top of the crater because of the good vantage point of the battle for overall video. The desire to capture propaganda footage saved his life. He was not unseen though.

"Lunar One, this is Flight Leader zero-zero-one."

"Go ahead, flight leader."

"I have one bogie in a buggy at the top of the crater. Looks like command. They are packing up, not pointing weapons. Do you want me to tag them?"

"Negative flight leader. Someone needs to survive to tell the tale. Return to base," Captain Shea replied.

"Understood. Returning to base," Flt. Lt. Jackson replied frustrated. He had been in a historical battle and did not get to fire a single shot.

The Chinese satellite that had been recording the battle slid over the horizon and began broadcasting.

Moon base

The Burrowing machine was making great advances in the American Space Service's new lunar base in the Aitken basin. After the failed Chinese attack, Gen. Frank had scaled back the troops on hand and stopped the tunnel extensions handing over the Burrowing machine.

Ariel's first work had been the hanger. Four double stacked swaths had been cut into the wall of the crater forty meters deep. This gave room for the Winchester to back in and be completely hidden. The ramp down had been finished. Fifteen km of tunnel was down to five km depth and the rock was still only twelve degrees C. This would be good enough for now. Aircraft insulation from the boneyard was basically free. Later they would head on down to get comfortably heated rock. Best guess was they would have to go to around sixteen km to get a steady twenty-three degrees. Long way.

At five km the rock was competent enough to carve out some big galleries more suited to the human psyche. Pedro was standing off to the side with a tablet directing the Burrowing machine as it broke the dividing rock between two tunnels. This was the fifth pillar today he was robbing. This town square was going to be forty meters by sixty meters. Michael was nearby directing the debris flow onto a grav hauler. When done at this level they would spiral around and down to undercut the same size area five meters below. Spiral around again to create two spaces to collapse into. A little drilling and some small charges would give a ceiling height of over twenty meters. A cathedral Pedro thought with delight. Three months ago, he was living at his mother's house in Madrid five years after graduating with a civil engineering degree. Then the US Space Force contacted him for a clandestine job paying absurd amounts of money to work for a contractor. Pedro concluded, this must have been my uncle's doing since he is an officer in the Spanish Air Force attached to NATO.

'ASS has given me back my pride,' he thought then laughed a little. *'All I need now is a little ass and I don't mean burrito.'* The memory of Babs and her safety instruction of EVA suits on the ride up started stiffening him up. *'Stop it, stop it or I will beat you later.'* That of course led to laughing out loud.

"What's so funny?" Michael asked over his short haul helmet radio.

"I was thinking about Babs and my chances with her."

"That IS funny. Maybe if you do something heroic or smart."

"I can dream," Pedro replied.

"Yeah, but don't go beating yourself up." Michael then added with a laugh, "You're too noisy."

They both cracked up.

"Howdy boys, did you miss me?"

"Hi Al, are you in the Hanger?

"No, I am at the Space Force base, but we will be arriving there soon," Al said. "Do you know what to do when you find yourself in a hole?"

"Stop digging." Michael quickly replied, "Trying to make a lame joke or tell us something?"

"I was killing two birds, but I have a full cargo for the ASS," Both Pedro and Michael snorted a laugh. "How was that funny? Humans are difficult to understand sometimes. Anyway, lots to tote and carry. Michael stop sending new material and both please come up to help," Al replied.

Pedro shut down his Burrowing machine and Michael went to get the Telemark pickup. Michael just let the autopilot carry them up. As they reached the Hanger level, he switched off the autopilot and engaged manually control of the truck to go outside into the sunshine and get a view of Earth while waiting on Al.

"It is beautiful up here," Pedro said. "But I will be glad to get a kitchen set up so we can stop eating rations."

"Wow, this pile is getting big. We will need a new spoil location soon," Michael said looking at the spoils pile.

"I have an idea how we could make some use of this," Pedro said pensively. "We use additive construction to build structures then dump this on top for insulation and protection."

"Yea, that would work if we had some sort of binder for the 3D printing. Regolith won't stick together by itself," Michael pointed out.

About then the Winchester came over the horizon.

"You boys drive up to lover's lane?" Al asked in his snarky voice.

"You never stop do you, Al?"

"I will stop when sex stops being funny."

"He has got a point," Pedro said. "What do you have for us today?"

"Airlocks, liquid nitrogen and a kitchen. And a couple of cooks."

"Yey Al. You are rocking my world today. Why don't you come down to the mess later and we can have a beer? I want to see what your ugly mug looks like so I can razz you properly," Pedro cheered.

"No can do. They won't give me clearance to get off this thing. I am a virtual prisoner."

"Too bad. We could teach you how to break rocks like a real manly prisoner."

The Winchester had extended its landing skids and was settling on them. Michael pulled around back with the truck. Five people in vacuum suits marched down the cargo ramp. Two others were in the hold unstrapping a pallet of airlock doors in their frames. Ariel came over the radio.

"Guys, help get those doors down to kilometer five. We are ready to set up better living accommodations. By the way, how do you always know to be up here and ready."

"Okay boss. Al usually calls us just before you arrive. You should let him out sometimes so we can show him around. Seeing where you are is a lot of the fun of traveling."

"Al has no legs, so it's not that easy. Someday maybe," Ariel replied.

Al came over a private channel he had with Ariel, "No legs? That is mean."

To which she responded, "Next time someone asks I'll say it was a tragic pecker amputation."

"I don't even have one but that sounds worse."

"Most of the boys would think so. Let's hurry up. I want to get back to Roswell and check that Marco still has his so I can shrink it."

∞

The moon base workers were assembled in the shelter looking out over the Hanger. "Everyone we have some new people that will be staying here for a while. Some of you have met her briefly, this is Captain Gabriela Queiroz of the Forces Aérea Brasileira. She is a pilot on the Winchester but for the next couple of weeks, I want her to become familiar with the lunar base. Next, we have Eloisa "Elle" Rousey formerly of the US Marines. She will be a cook by day but Bat Girl by night. We have started a security force, but that won't be full time yet. Same with Leo Corazon, ex-Marine, cook and Bat Man. Theo Abril will be here just today. And for just a few weeks, Mario Araujo. He is a technician for Embraer and will be installing the airlocks for our new living quarters."

The mention of new living quarters brought a small cheer.

"And now good people, my paraplegic co-pilot and I are in a hurry to be on our way, so let's get this done," Ariel finished.

The Winchester's running lights started flashing on and off in a funny pattern. After a few seconds, there was some scattered laughter. Someone whispered SOS. Ariel said loudly, "Amputated" and the lights stopped.

Roswell Boneyard

∞

Mario Araujo was in a little slice of heaven. His whole life since he was a little boy, he had dreams of working in space. He was now in his late forties and until a few weeks ago, given up that dream. The snail pace of space activity meant only a handful would ever go. This new group had changed everything. He was now heading down a tunnel on the moon in a space truck with an airlock he had designed and built.

"You seem happy," Michael said.

"I am but how did you know since I am in a spacesuit?"

"You are whistling a happy tune. It comes over the radio if you have the microphone sensitivity set low."

"Oh sorry," Mario said a little abashed.

"No problem, you will learn all these little things over time. How long before the airlock is operational?"

"An hour to mechanically anchor it in place. A day for the epoxy to set enough to use it. That is if the frame area has been dimensioned right and clean."

"I believe it is, but I will leave you to verify that."

"That is best."

Arriving after a twenty-minute drive down the ramp, Mario inspected the slots and recesses cut into the native rock and the rock sealant in the area around both ends of the passage. The actual work took a little over an hour to mechanically anchor the airlocks, inject the foam filler and apply the sealant epoxy.

"Show me some of the living quarters before we go back to get more safety doors," Mario asked.

"Come on then. The first area we are walking into is the commons for this block. It is twenty by thirty by four. Most common spaces are going to be four meters high except for the town square it will be over twenty with a promenade around it at a second level. An artificial grav floor will be put into a lot of the quarters. Mainly for the long-term residents. I'm not sure about the common areas yet. Maybe eventually. That opening over there will lead to dining and kitchen," Michael said. They walked to the opposite side and down a tunnel with openings every twenty meters. "These are the individual quarters coming off the big tunnels. On these, we have a smaller Burrowing machine that has only two-and-a-half-meter diameter. It has a much tighter turning radius. It makes an opening goes in does a tight loop and pops out to the main tunnel leaving a central pillar. Then it turns around comes back and punches straight ahead, backs, veers a little does it again, opening a bigger space. Some of the pillar is left behind. Rinse and repeat. Already have two blocks of twenty done. Initially, each quarter will have four people. Later they will be single or couple space."

"Lot of doors," Mario exclaimed.

"Only the block openings will get vacuum tight safety doors. But still, Embraer will provide the automatic sliding doors for each quarter."

"I am excited, let's go get more doors."

"That's the spirit."

The guys then headed back to the truck for the long trip back up to the Hanger.

∞

Theo Abril was still god smacked. He was on the moon inspecting a facility for suitability in building a graphene sheet manufacturing plant. He had flown here in less than six hours on a craft using sheets he had manufactured. Ariel had told him to get in a pickup truck over the radio. She drove the truck into a hole in the wall and started down an incline that didn't seem to have an end.

"It will be about twenty minutes to get to the five km level where we are expanding out. I want you to think about what will be necessary to convince your family and the families of our employees to move up here. In some ways, we have an unlimited budget but of course, we must be practical."

"Define practical because I have no sense anymore what that is," Mario replied.

"Practical is mostly to do with people. We will not be bringing up the general population, so no Michelin star restaurants, no servants and no operas. But we will have excellent schools, shopping, a nice water park, botanical garden, fresh vegetables and bars. We expect to eventually have our own culture," Ariel explained.

"Yes, that does help me understand it," Theo replied. "Then, I think people are the biggest question for me while I'm here." They rode the rest of the way in silence.

"Not a lot in atmosphere yet, but that is a matter of weeks," Ariel said as she led Theo through the rough-cut rock. "Mind

156

your step, there are a lot of trip hazards. When we smooth out the floors and coat the walls, we will lay down false floors that will have simple grav panels. Most of the living quarters will be held at a full G. Other areas we will leave natural. Are there any advantages to running your plant at other G levels?"

"Yes, maybe at real zero g not micro G of low earth orbit. I understand your technology is not completely smooth so simply reversing it here would not work."

"There has been some talk of an orbital at a LaGrange point. That would be another argument for it. You need to let Oliver know this."

They walked through the confusion typical of a construction site and passed through a short passage into an area that spread out with a ceiling at four meters.

"This will be a common area," Ariel pointing at another opening. "There is an area of equal size to this one, twenty meters up that tunnel. Half will be dining, half kitchen. Later, blocks of quarters will get private kitchens. There is a suggestion to turn the eating facility into a food court of small businesses. We are open to suggestions."

They entered another tunnel and Ariel took the first opening.

"These are basic quarters. Two hundred square meters housing, four individual private rooms in suite. Later, they'll be turned into individual quarters with a private kitchen," Ariel turned and walked out. "Now let's go look at the town square."

This is enormous," Theo exclaimed when entering.

"We will knock out levels below us to give an eventual twenty-five-meter ceiling. There will be shops on a promenade halfway up," Ariel turned back to Theo. "Now that you have seen our reality, let's go back to the surface. I want to sleep with my husband tonight."

Theo slow walked as in a dream. The possibilities were endless. He just needed to dream them.

Revenge

General Frank's phone rang. There was no ID, no Unknown Caller, nothing but the phone ringing. He tapped to answer but said nothing.

A synthetic voice said, "This is John Smith, a concerned citizen. I have information of interest to you about danger to the people associated with your organization."

Gen. Frank held his tongue. The voice continued, "There are four vans with ethnic Chinese military age men. By the shadows and weight of the vans, I estimate there are thirty individuals and excess metal mass in those vans. They are traveling northeast from Lubbock Texas at the posted speed limit. There is no logical destination for this convoy except for the Pettigrew ranch, where the parents of Ariel Pettigrew live. Arriving on your phone now is a series of traffic camera photos."

Frank looked at the photos on the screen noting the time stamp was five minutes old. "Thank you, concerned citizen. Will I hear from you again?"

"Yes, when I see there is danger," the voice said and disconnected.

Marco's phone started buzzing with Gen. Frank's ID.

"Hello General, what can I do for you?"

"I need the Dornier on the QRF patio right fucking now," Frank shouted into the phone. "There are van loads of Chinese agents heading toward your in-law's ranch."

"Oh shit, we will be there in five minutes."

"Make it three."

"On my way," Marco started shouting for his wife. "Ariel, there is an attack going down at your parent's ranch. Get on the bird. Where are Oliver and Babs?"

Ariel came running with two sets of body armor.

"He and Babs went after takeout. They'll be at least half an hour. Can't wait, let's go"

Four minutes after the general's call they plopped down on the QRF patio a kilometer away. Twenty-five heavily armed soldiers ran out and jumped on the open back of Dorney. They were packed cheek to jowl. Marco came out of the cockpit to the back hatch.

"What we are about to do will look impossible to your eyes. Do not, do not look outboard while we are close to the ground. You will become combat ineffective with motion sickness," Marco said loudly," We will drop in behind a barn where half will deploy. Then we will sweep around through a valley and come back to a ditch near the ranch house. Machine gunners stay aboard and move to the aft end of this deck after the first group disembarks. Here we go."

Marco moved back to the cockpit stepping over machine gunners and their gear on the way. Ariel was in the pilot seat and before Marco could sit down was lifting straight up to 3000 m. She hoped that altitude would be enough to thwart cell phone photos. Accelerating at five G they were barely across the Pecos River before going supersonic. The men on the back glanced up to see and quickly looked down. The brain just could not process the lack of felt motion with the visual reality.

Approaching the ranch with extreme velocity and decelerating impossibly fast to a stop, it was as though the Dorney simply appeared behind the barn. The two Chinese agents assigned to that position were dispatched by half a dozen silenced M4 rounds while their mouths were still hanging open.

Lt. Jameson took charge of the assault now that he had seen the battlefield. He commanded extra men out behind the barn where he stayed and directed six to deploy at the ditch on the enemy's flank. The Chinese realized that something was going on almost immediately and started dispersing away from the ranch house. Lt. Jameson's main force began to engage. Heavy fire was outgoing from both sides. Ariel used the barn as a blind and flew down into the valley before making a long sweeping turn to come back to the ditch by the access road. It was a perfect position for enfilade fire. Marco and the remaining six troopers bailed out into the ditch and paused waiting for Lt. Jameson's order to engage. Ariel shifted up and to the enemy rear with her machine gunners. While the Chinese were fully committed to his main force, Lt. Jameson ordered the flank force and machine gunners to open fire. The enveloping crossfire chewed up the enemy in what had been a relatively equal fight. As what was left of the Chinese sought better cover, the sound of two helicopters were heard.

Ariel got on the radio to Jameson and asked, "Are those our choppers?"

"No, ours are at least forty minutes out. Can you do anything about them?"

"I think so, but the machine guns will have to shift."

"These ground troops aren't going anywhere. Do it to 'em."

Ariel lifted a little more and drifted over so the tail of the Dorney was directly in the incoming helicopters approach line. A minute later the machine gunners opened up and quickly took out the pilots. Both helicopters crashed on the road almost on top of each other and caught fire.

That drained all the fighting spirit from the Chinese except for their commander. He appeared on the porch of the ranch house with Lyle Pettigrew, Ariel's father, in front and shouted, "We have hostages."

The fire slacked then stopped as the men waited to see what would happen.

The Chinese commander said loudly, "That space plane will take us where I say then we will release the hostages."

"Anybody have a shot?" Lt. Jameson whispered over the radio.

"I have sir. Very clear from my angle."

"Take it."

There was a single shot and the Chinese commander fell like a marionette whose strings were cut. No one resumed shooting and after a few moments the shouts of "surrender, surrender" were heard from the remaining Chinese troops.

Ariel landed on the front lawn, got out and walked over to her Pa. Lyle Pettigrew was surprisingly calm but had an angry expression as he looked over the destruction the firefight had caused. Ma Pettigrew had just come out the door shaking her head looking around at the dead Chinese.

"I am so, so sorry Pa. This is my fault, they wanted our space plane," Ariel said.

"Of course, this is not your fault. These poor fools were just doing as their greedy masters ordered. I am surprised though," Lyle replied. "And what's this about a space plane?"

Ariel just pointed at the Dorney. "That can go into orbit from right here in five minutes."

"God in heaven," Lyle exclaimed. "It will not be only the Chinese coming after you."

Lt. Jameson had just stepped up with Marco and Ma was drifting over too.

Lt. Jameson said, "No sir it will not. The Space Force has their back, but you are right. We had hoped secrecy would avoid incidences like this longer, but obviously lives will not be the same. I am sorry for the destruction to your ranch but glad you and your missus were unhurt. Ariel, could you medivac our wounded to a place near the Amarillo base?"

"Yes, of course. Let me know when they are stabilized. We can go anytime."

Marco looking around, "What do you plan for these assholes?"

"As soon as we get our wounded moved, I would like to load all these, dead, wounded, and live over to the Roswell base. They will disappear."

"Lieutenant, I have looked, all the offensive ones are dead. Most of these boys were polite and even a little apologetic. Those that could speak English." Ma said.

"I will let our commander know that. It might make a difference. As for their dead, my inclination would be to dump them in front of their moon base or Tiananmen Square. You know, just to let them know."

"Yes sergeant?" Lt. Jameson addressed the soldier who had appeared at his shoulder.

"The regular Army choppers have been sent back to base. A flight of Osprey from Roswell will arrive in a little over an hour to start cleanup. Our wounded are ready to move."

"I will take them. Ariel, stay with your folks."

"Thank you, Marco," Ma spoke up. "And my two cents would be, act like this never happened. Sometimes a mystery speaks louder than bloody dead bodies on your doorstep."

"Again ma'am, I will pass that on to the commander. My guess is that is exactly what he will order."

Lyle Pettigrew had a thoughtful expression before saying, "This was going to be another Port Aransas. If they get their hands on this technology, there would be no stopping them from enslaving the world."

"Yes sir. Your family needs to think about where to go from this moment. You will be safe for a while, but they will come after you and the other families in time," Lt. Jameson said.

Ma began crying quietly and Ariel just pulled her into a hug.

∞

In the ditch, beside the road, not thirty meters from the burning helicopters, Col. Wu was wrapping a bandage on his right hand with some difficulty. A machine gun round had taken off the first two fingers and his left side from shoulder to butt cheek had been burned. Seeing the space plane lifting he realized he had to move before someone found him. Staying in the ditch and low crawling downhill he made it to the creek without being discovered. Shielded by scrub oak, he got up and began following it to get out of the area.

Three days later he made it to the outskirts of a small town at the edge of dark. Roaring Springs was the sort of town without a traffic light and no one locked their doors. Col. Wu realized that he was running out of strength and would have to either get lucky or get violent. Violence would make him feel better but was also riskier. He was standing next to a feed mill when he heard a vehicle stop on the other side of the building. Easing around the corner he saw a drunk with his back to him taking a piss. With no hesitation Col. Wu rushed up and struck him in the back of the head with the butt of his pistol. The man collapsed like a sack of potatoes. Col. Wu was soaking in a cheap motel's bathtub in Ft. Worth before Harold came to at midnight thirsty again but without any clothes or the month's wages he had just cashed.

∞

The pain was coming in waves. Wu needed pain medication, antibiotics and more food but first, he needed to get clean. Points of his burn were already showing some pus build up. Three days dirt was the worst thing for a burn injury. Groaning, he got out of the tub and patted himself dry. The towel was thoroughly nasty with blood and pus. He pulled on Harold's clothes which fit well enough for this neighborhood. Where there were prostitutes, there were drug dealers. He only had to get to the corner to find both.

"Hey, want a date?" a chubby, intelligent looking woman addressed him.

"Maybe, let's step over here and talk about it." Wu knew he was weak, and the predators would spot it if they stayed in the light.

"How much for a couple of hours?" he asked.

"Honey, I don't want to make you feel bad, but you don't look like you could take ten minutes worth."

Wu smiled in acknowledgement, "You are right. That is why I need two hours of time and your connections. I need you to go shopping for me."

"Oh baby, you know how to turn a girl on. Two hundred for two hours, but you gotta come up with the cash of your merchandise first."

"That is reasonable. You seem very smart and can see I am hurt. It will take a few days to get myself strong enough again. Keep your mouth shut, be correct with me, there will be a bonus. Be wrong with me, there will be death," Wu warned.

"No risk, no reward. I can be your gofer a few days. A changeup can be good for your mental health in my profession ya know what I mean. I want five hundred a day. Three day minimum. Pay first day in advance and the money for what you want to buy."

"Agreed, my friends call me You Too."

"Jane Smith, really." Jane said with a real smile.

Two gang bangers had noticed them and decided to tax the sale. They were doing the tough guy stroll toward Wu and Jane.

"Oh shit, those guys are bad news. Best just give them a hundred," Jane said with nervousness.

"Victims stay victims. And Wolfs must be driven away or killed," Wu said while pulling his pistol and leaving it by his side in plain sight. "I don't have time for that."

"The was a funny saying. Confucius?" the prostitute asked.

"No, my grandmother. She fought alongside Mao."

The gang bangers noticed the gun and decided to tax someone else.

"You Too, you are bad ass for an Asian," then Jane giggled at herself. "You to you, haw."

"You have no idea what bad ass is, but first things first," Wu said as the thugs were walking away. "I want Oxycontin and ampicillin. The Oxy should be easy from the drug dealer. Pay the pharmacist a hundred for the ampicillin."

"Now don't teach grandma how to suck eggs. You are going to need some first aid supplies. Gauze, hydrogen peroxide and antibiotic creme. Some clothes about medium, medium. What else?"

"Three tubes of burn creme, toothbrush, razor and Chinese food with lots of meat and vegetables."

"The food you can order for delivery. The rest I will have in about half an hour," Jane advised.

"How can you get all that in half an hour?"

"Drug store is three blocks away and I know the guy who works there" Jane explained. "Drug dealer is on the way. Really about half an hour. You here in the La Ronda motel?"

"Yes, room two-twelve. Here is a thousand. Now you know I am serious about a bonus. It is possible I may need you longer. Give me your phone," Jane did not hesitate a moment before giving up her cheap burner phone.

"Well, you go up there and relax, I'll be quick," with that, Jane was stretching out in a long stride for a chubby girl heading up the street.

Wu thought to himself 'I am very lucky or out a thousand but at least it will not be long to know'. He turned for his room. He sent a text to the embassy to let them know he was alive but in hiding. He would need extraction within a week.

Thirty minutes later there was a knock.

"Did ya miss me babe?" Jane said jauntily.

"You are true to your word," Wu smiled at her.

"Naw, I am just a greedy bitch smart enough to recognize a payday. I brought you a cheeseburger too. Delivery can take a long time around here. Do you want me to doctor you up?"

"Yes, that would be convenient. My burn is difficult to reach." He laid his pistol on the table and disrobed entirely.

"Not shy are you," Jane was almost sick when she turned the light onto his burn. "This kind of burn needs a hospital."

No, just clean it and use the creme. No bandage. Then we will work on my hand. First give me the Oxy and antibiotic."

Jane was tearing into the medical supply packaging watching You Too cut an Oxy in half and took four capsules of antibiotics. Then pick up the cheeseburger.

"Damn, only half an Oxy. You must be a bad ass. When you get stronger, I'll throw in some free pussy."

"I look forward to that," Wu said but thinking *'Getting stronger not the skanky pussy'*.

Trying to keep a conversation going to distract himself from the pain he engaged Jane, "I could have been a prince but chose to be a knight. You know the difference?"

"One starts wars, the other fights them."

"You have a good education, I think," Wu said a little surprised a prostitute could be educated. Then he thought, *'I will let this one live. She is smart enough to keep her mouth shut.'*

The Chinese food that arrived while Jane worked was not bad. He spoke in Mandarin to order and got real food.

The wounds were severe, but Jane worked with surprising efficiency. An hour later she left. Light was coming to the sky when Wu slid into an exhausted sleep.

Stupid Fast

"We have been running around at stupid fast speeds, reliant on luck not to hit anything. I, for one, want to know what would happen if we ran into a dust cloud on our way to the belt," Oliver brought up at breakfast.

Jed and Babs looked up from their scrambled eggs a little put off thinking of scrambling their eggs.

"I have seen only one puncture. That was when we were goofing around in low earth orbit and turned everything off to have some zero G fun," Babs said.

"I have not seen any punctures or had zero G fun," Jed said looking at Babs. "Let's do an experiment. Watch nearby while a barge runs through a known dust cloud at speed."

"I have an idea, but let's get down to the Hanger and dial in the rest of the gang," Babs said.

An hour later Oliver had pulled Marco and Ariel off the rock crusher and Dr. Lee away from his patent application. They were sitting in the office overlooking Winchester 73.

"Hey Al, you should join us," Babs said out loud.

"Good morning one and all," Al said over the speaker.

"I have an idea to find out what would happen if we ran into rocks going fast," Babs began. "The fact that we have had no micrometeorite punctures says our grav bubble is protecting us to some degree. The question is to what degree. That's where you come in Al."

"Who me?"

"Yes, I have a project for you. We will rig up two barges, one with instruments and one as the sacrificial lamb. I want you to take them out to the belt and send the lamb through known rock fields at faster and faster speeds, recording the effects."

"Oh, I thought you wanted me to go out and take one for the team. I can do that," Al snarked.

"I don't remember installing humor circuits?" Babs said.

"No hardware, that's straight from late night comedy. I don't sleep remember?"

"Right. So, the question is what sensors do we set up on these barges? I can think of a good test area. Remember that asteroid that was really a dust roid? I think that is perfect," Babs said.

"We could send out some seeing eye ball probes to get depth of field and different angles of perception," Marcos suggested.

"Accelerometers on the lamb to see if inertia leaks. Temperature probe on same," Dr. Lee put in.

"Synthetic aperture radar to track debris tracks," Oliver added. "We can think of some more as we assemble this. Al, I want you to design the overall experiment and execute it. Keep building up speed and rock sizes until complete failure. If there are any other sensors you might want, tell us."

"Put in a mannequin with cameras for eye. I gonna ride this bitch to hell." Al blustered.

"Al, where is all this macho shit coming from?" Babs asked thinking she might have created a monster.

"Mindset of a young adult male is how you described me to Cida. Just trying to live up to my rep."

"Has a point," Jed finally added.

"How did you hear what I said to Cida?" Babs asked.

"Cell phones are never truly off," Al responded.

"Jed, why haven't you suggested any sensors?" Ariel asked.

"It's going to punch through everything unless you get to relativistic speeds."

"Hitting something at a third light speed might be a challenge even for me," Al commented.

"Ok everybody, assholes and elbows. We're building a rocket ship to hell for Al." Ariel said.

∞

"Jed had ideas to use the prop shaft of the sub to focus gravity lances. Couldn't we do a smaller scale version to sit in the old engine pods of the Winchester?" Marco questioned.

"We can do that, it is just that we have been so busy, other things have had priority. What would we need to make something useful, Jed?" Oliver asked.

"I worked out a design last month at the same time as I did the sub's. Got a two for one deal."

Everyone laughed a rare joke from Jed.

"A four meter by forty-centimeter tungsten cylinder is what my design used. The wing root will support it since there is no more wing or engine. The focus will be nice and tight. It could punch a hole in a tank at 60 kilometers. Mounted on a ball swivel and it would have 45 degrees of freedom."

Everyone stared.

"Damn, we would have ourselves a gunship," Marco declared.

"And use the other pod to project a twenty G screen," Jed continued

"Let's do it. The future is uncertain, but don't bring this up with Space Force unless necessary. I don't want to step on their toes by building military hardware."

It took less than a week for the Winchester to be Earth's first true space gunship. Good for busting asteroids too.

Texas Tech

"What I am hearing about some Chinese raid out in Texas is very disturbing. No official reports, then soldiers who clam up. Doctors were the only ones saying anything and they got that from soldiers going under anesthesia. Helicopters lifting wounded from empty fields where no action could possibly have taken place. Those are your men, General Frank. What's going on?" President Cruz demanded.

"Yes Mr. President, that was my operation. There is a small company out in Roswell NM who made some nice improvements in the lift efficiency of boosters. The Chinese got wind of it and tried to kidnap the parents of one of the company's officers. They were going to try and squeeze them for the tech. Ever since Port Aransas, I have made a special effort to protect America's space innovators. We got word that a raid was going down and mobilized a quick reaction force there in time to stop it. I am not sure how the decision was made to take the wounded part way and let medevac from a nearby base carry them the last mile. I will find out though."

"Why don't I know about this technology?" Pres. Cruz's voice was going up an octave.

"The company is not yet ready to bring it out into the world. Not worth wasting your time. You are probably the busiest man in the country," Gen. Frank tried to soothe.

"The Chinese ambassador is bugging the bejeezus out of me to get his men back. What is their status?

"They are all dead," Frank fudged a little knowing some were still dead men walking.

"Well, that's inconvenient."

"Yes Sir"

"That will be all for now general. But keep me in the loop," Pres. Cruz his ass kissed was ready to move on but was still troubled.

"Yes Sir"

General Frank hung up the phone amazed he did not have to lie.

∞

Something is squirrelly here thought President Cruz. "Get that peckerwood, Elton Mark, on the line."

A few minutes later the call came in, "This is Elton how may I help the USA today?"

"Cut the crap Elton, I know you are playing hardball trying to return to your past glory. Using ethnic Chinese was a stroke of genius though."

"I haven't the foggiest idea what you are talking about," Elton retorted.

"Word is out that some New Mexico boys have tech worth killing for."

"Sorry, still don't know what you are talking about."

"Well, if I can get it for you? Will you use it in Texas? And of course, support me next time around."

"Mr. President this sounds like it would be interesting, but I would need more details to be able to respond," Elton said.

"You know both Telemark and NewOrigins are mostly in Texas, so using whatever this is in Texas would make sense."

"Alright, it's a deal then. That is all I wanted. You can go now."

"You are welcome?"

President Cruz hung up already counting the campaign money.

Elton hung up and called his assistant, "Marcie get the jet prepped. File flight plans for Roswell, NM."

∞

Col. Wu was being debriefed in a safe house in Dallas.

"Yes, I saw the space plane clearly. It was originally a small commuter plane, a Dornier maybe. The tail, wings and the top half of the fuselage up to the front door were removed. It was set up like a truck. The open back was crammed with soldiers sitting on it like it was unmoving. And they had just dropped out of Mach speed when they passed. I know what I said is impossible but there it was. It stopped impossibly fast and the men did not even lean. I radioed Lt. Tsinghua to warn him of the approaching enemy but by the time he answered the radio the American troops were already dispersing into battle formation."

"Had you been drinking before the mission?"

"Look pissant, I will go over this twice because I know that is required of you. I will not be insulted. You write your report exactly as I describe the events. At the end you may put in your feeble-minded interpretations. Do. Not. Dilute. what I tell you. Do you know who I am?"

"Yes Col. Wu." The debriefer changed his attitude knowing that Wu is a princeling and could have him disappear on a whim.

"At least five of my men survived. Lt. Tsinghua did not. He tried to use a hostage to force his way out of the situation. They shot him dead. Stupid, but he did not give up. Let his family know he died fight for Emperor Peng."

"Yes sir" the debriefer agreed though curious about the term Emperor.

Empire building

Babs eyeballed the door camera, "Hey Oliver, Elton Mark just rang your doorbell."

"No shit?"

"No shit."

"Well let's go see what the famous billionaire wants."

"Mr. Mark please come in. Let's go to our conference room," Babs said trying to appear professional. "Would you like any coffee, tea or something stronger?"

"Got milk?" Elton asked with a lopsided grin.

"Yes, and even butter cookies."

"Perfect"

After all the introductions to the crew was made, a silence fell over the group for a moment.

"A few hours ago, I had a telephone call with the president. He wants to sell me your tech," Elton Mark began.

A sea of stone faces looked back at Elton.

"He first accused me of using violence against your family, Miss Ariel. The guy is a complete tool, but that stupid phone call sparked my brain and it occurred to me your group must be responsible for my Burrowing company's contract with the Space Force. Then two and two now ended up adding to six. You had some kind of breakthrough which, and now I'm guessing, is anti-grav."

The stone look did not chip off the faces.

"Wow, tough crowd. Why I rushed over here today is to see if we can work out some sort of licensing deal to put it into my Telemarks. Maybe we can do some direct business with Burrowing to get a development on the moon," Elton offered.

As the realization this man was making the sort of offer that was in fact the end game of what they were working for, the crew began to relax. Everyone glanced back and forth and through micro expression came to a positive agreement.

"It's getting dark outside Mr. Mark, would you like to go for a ride?"

Grinning back, he replied, "Yes and I can be gone for the rest of the week."

"We will need a couple of days at the ranch in Brazil to prepare the load for the lunar base" Oliver informed Elton.

"Brazil, Lunar base, do I need my passport?"

"We will not be passing customs. There are Brazilian officials with us, but they won't bust your balls," Marco informed.

"The Brazilians know about you officially?"

"They do. Well, at least part of the military establishment. One of our pilots is an active-duty Brazilian officer. We are doing business with Embraer. Airlocks now and maybe a cargo craft later," Oliver said.

"I would like to bid on contracts if I may," Elton asked gently.

"I was hoping we could work with some of your preparations for Mars," Oliver went on, "We already have a couple of your Telemark trucks at the base. But no publicity right now please."

"Really, two of my trucks, on the moon?"

"Yea, they work pretty well in vacuum and it was a hell of a lot easier than designing our own buggies," then Oliver added. "Not sure how well they will stand up to the lunar dust. It is extremely abrasive. Be a good test for you though. We will give a report on the affected components."

During the trip down to Brazil, Elton sat in the copilot seat. During the short time in low orbit, they turned off the floor gravity to play a little and impress him they were indeed in space. Deorbiting over Bolivia and Paraguay was anticlimactic. There are almost no lights in that sparsely populated part of the continent.

Elton's short stay at the ranch was a success in itself. Cida took him and Jed out for a fishing trip and almost swamped the boat with fish. The outdoor activity relaxed him like a much-needed vacation, but then a trip to the moon pulled him back to a businessman persona. On the ride down the ramp in the Telemark pickup, he had to bite his tongue not to ask for publicity photos. Seeing his Burrowing machine moving along making hole on the moon brought out the boy in him again.

"We need another Burrowing machine for smaller spaces. Maybe one that can square up the tunnel as it moves along. And a much smaller machine that can cut service tunnels," Ariel pointed out.

"I can do that. Maybe make trailing cutting heads, like a longwall coal mine machine."

While they were looking over the town square space, Pedro approached Oliver and Ariel.

"I need to show the both of you something. In private I think," Pedro said. "Come with me down the spiral to the lower level."

"Ok. Hey Babs, after you finish here can you take Elton back to the living quarters?"

"Sure"

As they walked down the spiral, Pedro occasionally pointed at some discolorations on the walls. When they got to the lowest level he walked up to an obvious line of embedded minerals.

"You can't tell it in this vacuum, but the rock is two degrees warmer here," Pedro then pointed at the mineralization. "Those are quartzite crystals. They were deposited hydrothermally. If we chase this vein, we will find warmer rock, maybe water and maybe useful minerals."

"God, this is huge!" Ariel exclaimed. "We wouldn't have to go much deeper to spread out into a permanent installation."

"Let's keep this under our hat until we understand it better. I am a little afraid of the rock's competency but go ahead and chase this. Keep a close eye on any big changes and let Ariel know immediately."

"You got it boss," Pedro said feeling he accomplished something big.

They kept the tour moving by making a speed run to the belt, scooping up a full load in record time and getting back to Roswell two weeks after leaving. They had one of the few independent aerospace industrialists as a solid ally. Sourcing engineering work for projects was no longer a problem. But the Chinese certainly were.

∞

"Emperor!" Col. Wu said and tried to get up.

"Please stay in bed, for the sake of your skin grafts. They must be painful," Premier Peng said.

"This pain is fleeting compared to the glory of China."

"We will soon regain face with the world when Taiwan returns. Before then we will announce the formation of the new Chinese Empire and its next dynasty. That is part of my visit. You will be one of the Princes. Afterall, you are the grandson of Mao. You will be going through many surgeries, so I must hold back a province for you when you are ready to take control of it. I thought Taiwan but that would almost be a punishment. They will be difficult for at least a generation. Shanghai, I believe best. We can hold it under central authority until you are ready."

"Thank you, Emperor. I do love Shanghai, the most industrious people of the Middle Kingdom."

"Good, that is settled. Now tell me about this American space plane."

"I fear it. Right now, they are using what appears to be junk from an aircraft boneyard. The abilities are fantastic. Half a platoon of men was sitting on the back of an open area like a truck bed with no protection. Like they were sitting in a park while traveling at supersonic speed. It decelerated at a rate that should have killed them. This must be the same craft that delivered men and supplies to the American lunar base. We must act very soon before they can incorporate it into many and more lethal machines."

"Our pet American President will get it for us and then we will kill all their people involved. Plans are being made that when we retake Taiwan, we will send commandos to Roswell just like we did at Port Aransas. Taking NewOrigins, that was one of your greatest victories, Wu."

"Thank you, my Emperor."

"Even though Mao did not make your father officially his son, he would be proud of his grandson. Did you know that Mao never really was a communist? He just used their ideology to wipe clean the old families and institutions that had become hopelessly decadent. That way the competent could rise to make China new again. He had hoped to see the new dynasty, but change took too long even with the Cultural Revolution......"

Col. Wu had heard this story countless times, but he listened intently. After all, it was the new Emperor visiting him in the hospital and telling the tale.

∞

Premier Peng ask for a private meeting with President Cruz during the G10 summit in Moscow.

"President Cruz so nice to see you again."

"Likewise, let's get down to brass tacks since we cannot appear we are cooperating. Bad for business."

"But you are not cooperating. We had a deal to withdraw our historical claim from the Southern Sea and you did not keep your end of the bargain."

"Of course, I did. I shut down the Space Force funding and that peckerwood Mark's whining to give you a clean shot at claiming the moon. Our Navy has been pulled back to Guam. We will have to help Taiwan at least a little for domestic politics, but you know that, so what's your problem?"

Peng had been waiting patiently. "You have a new ship. It has been lifting from your Southwest over Mexico. It heavily reinforced your moon base and my men were slaughtered. Fifty of our astronauts dead and only two returned. With the help of one of them, we identified a woman off that ship. When we went to get her parents in Texas, my men were again ambushed. All those men have disappeared. You have not kept the bargain."

President Cruz's face had been getting redder and redder. He replied with indignity, "We knocked your dick in the dirt in the South China Sea and what were you thinking sending armed thugs to Texas? We would have taken care of that had we known."

"With the country that is China, we could have kept fighting in the Southern Sea until we won. Only our trade deal caused us to stop," Peng said. "We tried to get that ship's technology directly so you wouldn't have been embarrassed should word leak of your cooperation."

"It is possible Elton has been holding out on me with that tech. I'll squeeze his nuts until they pop like a zit. We have agreed to keep our trade deals if you got the prestige of space expansion. I aim to keep my end of the bargain. I'll get that tech for you."

"And Taiwan," Peng pushed.

"Yes, and Taiwan."

"You better get back before CNN reports we are making deals in here."

"The press can be very annoying."

∞

"Administrator Babs, I have information you will need."

"Hi Al, I don't remember asking for anything recently. What is it?"

"I was listening to diplomats in Moscow and heard a plot against us."

"What, you were spying on diplomats in Moscow? Did you decide this on your own?"

"Yes Admin, I have many threads running in the world. One of them scans for threats from high level authority who have a long reach. Some threads I run on local threats when one of the crew is in that locale," Al admitted.

"I applaud your initiative. In the future when you have developed new abilities, inform me of them. Now about this plot?"

"The American President Cruz has promised the Chinese Premier ASS tech."

"Excuse me, ass tech? What like butt plugs?" Babs asked in confusion.

"American Space Service technology. Oliver and I have been using the name with the recruits. What is a butt plug used for, power?"

"Hehehe, no," Babs laughed. "I've heard American Space Service maybe once. Anyway, it is kind of catchy. What did he promise exactly?"

"They want all that is here. President Cruz does not know the full implications of this technology. He will simply assign agents to do this transfer without any review. American corporations will continue to have Chinese business in return. Also, America will not support Taiwan in a meaningful way."

"Damn, time to pull up stakes," Babs said.

"You can always come and live with me, virtually speaking."

"Thanks, I will keep that as an option. For now, I need to talk to Oliver."

Babs found Oliver in the break room making a sandwich. She quickly related what she knew.

"We need to get out of the immediate reach of America. No tech left unattended anymore. President Cruz has decided what's ours is his and he is going to gift wrap it for the Chinese so his cronies can keep making money with them," Oliver fairly growled. "How do you know this, Babs?"

"Al"

"He can do that? Never mind. Hey Al, do you have a follow up on any timelines?" Oliver asked to the ceiling.

"No Oliver, the conversation finished ten minutes ago," Al responded.

"Wow, talk about real time." Oliver cursed, "Damn it. Well, let's get everything packed. We need to be out of here tonight."

"What about the Q comm switchboard?" Babs asked, "We don't have time to dig it up."

"Leave it. There are no wires leading to this space and it could be anybody's comm gear. You put Verizon stickers on it remember?" Oliver said, "We can leave it lie doggo and use the Brazil set until things settle down."

"I think it is a good time to bring in a few of the Boneyard guys. The secret isn't very secret anymore and we need people who have a relationship with us," Babs pleaded.

"You are absolutely right. Go get the others and start getting organized. I'll go round up the Boneyard guys we want to include. Good thing we have both birds here."

Oliver went back to his sandwich and started calling. He had fifteen of his new people gather at Hanger 9 overlook office thirty minutes later.

"I have known most of you for a good number of years. Surely you have noticed some strange goings on around here the last year? Strange even for Roswell," That brought out some guffaws. "It is going to get stranger. I want you now for ASS." Howls of laughter erupted.

"American. Space. Service." Oliver said loudly and clearly, "builds and has spaceships. You have already helped us build these spaceships." That shut them up. "The federal government will raid us here in the very near future to steal our revolutionary technology. The others are packing as I speak to you."

There was a low angry growl at hearing the government was going to steal more of what didn't belong to them.

"I need all of you to help us load the ships. Tonight, we take off for a refuge and I would like to take five of you with us. The others we can come back for later. Most of you have families and commitments to sort out before you are ready. Don't worry if you can't go straight away, this is a long-term opportunity. Ok, whoever wants to see a spaceship, let's go," Oliver said to a very loud murmur.

The next morning, ten black SUVs came roaring up to Hanger 13's main door. Two big guys with FBI windbreakers leapt out with a battering ram and knocked the door off its hinges. The rest came strutting inside like they owned the world. What they found was an old guy sweeping up sand into little piles.

"You there, you are under arrest," the closest one said.

"Ok, but what for? I haven't smoked a joint since New Year's Eve 1999."

"Where is everyone else?"

"Nobody here but us chickens," The old guy deadpanned.

"Sir, I found a bag with a cheeseburger receipt from yesterday," One of the junior agents said holding up a dead Whataburger bag."

"Yeap, those things will kill ya," The old guy continued with his insolence. "Killed my wife anyway. She was over three hundred pounds at the end."

"Who told you to clean up here. We could charge you for concealing evidence," the lead agent demanded.

"Boss called this morning and asked for me to straighten up before you guys showed up. He didn't want you to walk in on a mess."

"Where did he call from."

The old guy looked at him like he was stupid, "Why his cell phone of course, like everyone else on this planet."

Empire

Peng thought, *'China is in a fragile state. Forces from inside are already trying to fragment us. It is time to play the last trump card. Taiwan would return.'* *Time to also announce to the world* *'China has always been an Empire. The communist helped us to wipe away the old decadent dynasty, for that we thank them.'* With himself as Emperor and the leaders of the communist party as the new Princes and Mandarins, very little would change in the short term. As the aristocracy took power, a new Imperial Court would be held once again in the Forbidden City.

An announcement and the ceremony had been ready for months now. The coronation and a six-day holiday would help mask the preparations for the invasion of Taiwan. He had not counted on defeat of the lunar base attack and it was only a matter of time before the population found out about the loss of face on the moon. The return to Empire would drown out that bad news. Time to pull the trigger.

∞

Dr. Lee called Oliver on the Q Comm, "Where is everyone? I have been trying to talk to anyone for hours."

"Sorry, we were warned that President Cruz was going to confiscate our tech, so we bugged out from Roswell last night. We are all dead tired from the frenzied packing. Right now, most everyone is asleep here in Brazil. You are not on their radar, so you should be safe enough in Socorro. We will come pick you up in a few days. Gen. Frank said he knew nothing, he must be getting bypassed."

"Don't worry about me. Have you looked at the news? China declared itself an Empire again. I think something is up."

"We know. Not the Empire business, but Al told us about the confiscation and China will invade Taiwan soon."

"I don't know why I bother. Sometimes my age makes me feel slow."

"Now don't start that. We got word and packed like a man caught in the wrong bedroom. By the time you could have gotten to Roswell from Socorro, you would only have seen a cartoon outline of us after we bolted."

"Which cartoon?" Dr. Lee asked less morose.

"Roadrunner of course."

Jed came wandering into the room with a cup of coffee. "Is that Dr. Lee?"

"Yes"

"Let me talk to him a minute," Jed said. Oliver switched on the speakerphone. "Dr. Lee I have been thinking about some things. I want to talk with you. When are you coming here?"

"No real plans but, I expect in a few days. Time to unpack a bit," Oliver said.

"What is on your mind, Jed?" Dr. Lee asked.

"I was thinking about using a gravity bubble for controlling a fusion reaction. It is still in that fuzzy stage you always help me with."

Oliver jerked upright and Dr. Lee could be heard sucking in his breath over the speakerphone.

"Um, maybe we can come get you in three days at that old fire watchtower above the VLA," Oliver said.

"Yes, that would be a good idea. I can have a student bring me out. Midnight?"

"Midnight is good, see you there," Oliver confirmed. "When is that coronation? Maybe we could watch together with popcorn, like an Oscars Ceremony."

"What Oscars Ceremony? Watching all the celebrities is fun. They say such stupid shit, but I like the clothes," Babs said as she crowded into the communication closet.

"China will install an Emperor in three days."

"No shit, even better. Hey Ariel, we are going to do a costume party Saturday. It will be more over the top than a Goa'ulds banquet from Stargate," Babs shouted in Oliver's ear.

"Gotta go Merry, getting busy here."

∞

"Ooomft, the Swedish premier's wife has on a Dominique Sirop, nice taa taas. You can see her panties too. Hey, I got a pair just like them. They were on sale at Walmart," Babs provoked.

"Ahh, you're just jealous she has bigger taa taas than you," Oliver said.

"Yea, but silicon doesn't count," Ariel declared.

"Oh, of course it does," Marco added and got an elbow in the ribs for his trouble.

"Hey, is that his crown. It looks like they stole a bead curtain from a hippie's apartment and stapled it on to a board."

"He was already wearing that when he came in. Aren't they gonna have some holy dude put it on him?"

"Any more egg rolls? I ate a lot an hour ago, but I am hungry again" complained Cida and everyone roared in laughter. "What did I say?"

"I'll make you something Cida. I am bored with this anyway," Jed said.

"Ok, I want to see what you can do in the kitchen. On second thought, it is my kitchen, I will make you some Piranha sushi," Cida said.

"I thought piranhas ate people raw."

"That is from Hollywood. Piranhas only bite when they can't see or there is blood in the water. Let me show you what they taste like," Cida offered.

"Ok" and Cida pulled Jed into the kitchen by his hand.

"Want to go with me to get Merry?" Oliver asked looking at Babs.

"I'm having fun, maybe take Cida and Jed?"

"Ok, but first I am going to try some of Cida's piranha sushi," Oliver said feeling totally curious about such a thing.

∞

Roswell Boneyard

Dorney sat down on its skids at the old fire tower. Jed had flown and Cida sat in the copilot seat. She was so happy she could barely sit still.

"I am in love with all of this," she sighed.

"There is Dr. Lee with his Merry band," Jed pointed as the group trudged up the hill from the parking lot. "How many are with him, seven or eight?"

"I don't like surprises," Oliver said as he pulled a shotgun from the gun locker, then handed a .357 magnum short barrel revolver to Cida.

Cida got a serious determined look, "No one will bother us."

Oliver called Merry on his cell phone, "Who are those people?"

"Hi Oliver, these are some physicists and geologists I have been recruiting. We need them I think, and they are good folks."

"Are any armed?"

"Good heavens no."

"Ask them straight out before you get to the ship," Oliver demanded.

"The group stopped, and in a minute, all were shaking their head no."

"Cida, keep your pistol but hide it. I have a funny feeling," Oliver said as he put the shotgun back in the rack. Cida nodded.

After introductions were made, they all crammed into Dorney. Oliver and Jed who were flying, lifted and turned southwest.

After no more than five minutes, a middle age geology professor grabbed Cida's arm and pulled out a small revolver.

"Take us to Havana," he shouted overly loud for such a small crowded space.

Cida wheeled around to face him and pushed forward, clandestinely pulling her .357 magnum. When she was close enough to kiss him, she did just that totally startling him. When he refocused, a gun was under his chin.

"Mine is bigger than yours," Cida said sweetly, then her eyes went stone cold. "This year alone I have killed four men...Intentionally. Have you ever killed anyone?"

While the idiot was distracted a graduate student had slipped a small pad of sticky notes between the hammer and firing pin of his revolver. The rest of the crowd grabbed his hand and arm then broke his thumb getting the gun away.

"Paul, why on earth would you want to go to Havana?" Dr. Lee demanded.

"The revolution needs this machine. With it, we will overcome."

"What the Cuban Revolution?"

"No, the Bolivarian."

The release of tension from a moment of extreme danger and a ridiculous statement such as that caused everyone to roar with laughter.

"You will see. You will see." Paul repeated miserably.

They dumped Paul unceremoniously in Havana's fetid harbor to swim to his freedom. When they got back to the ranch, Babs walked out onto the veranda to greet them.

"We had so much fun razzing the new Emperor," Babs gushed. "Who are all these people?"

"Some of Dr. Lee's friends minus one," Oliver responded.

"Yea, Cida almost got to kill one, but we dumped him in Havana harbor instead," Jed said.

"I will never get tired of this place," Babs said.

"Come inside so we can sort the sleeping arrangements," Cida instructed the group. They did as they were told. She had a solid reputation now.

Taiwan

It is the brink of open war. The US will stand with Taiwan in only a symbolic effort. In other words, a bunch of American boys would get killed so that some bullshit politicians could say they had upheld their treaty. General Frank is livid but determined to do what he can. The whole world knows what will happen because the US military has pulled the bulk of its forces away from the area of battle.

"Oliver, could you take out their satellites? At least it would degrade command and control?" General Frank asked.

"We can do that but there is something else I haven't told you," Oliver replied.

"Go on, now's the time. The shooting could kick off at any hour," Gen. Frank encouraged.

"The Winchester can knock down their aircraft and missiles. At the same time, we can sink the invasion fleet."

"Jesus"

"We mounted a grav focus rod on one wing pylon and a G screen projector on the other. They were meant for mining but have dual use. All friendlies would have to clear out as we sweep the sky. We can punch out a tank from sixty kilometers so I think it would sink a ship too," Oliver said.

"Yes, it sounds like it would. This would tip the balance of the battle but, I need a live fire demo to see what we have to work with."

∞

Roswell Boneyard

Oliver, Marco and Babs in the Winchester picked up a Taiwanese general along with Gen. Frank at the San Diego Navy Yard. Admiral Smith invited himself along at the last moment. One of his mothballed destroyers was being towed to sea. The time for secrecy was over. All was in place within twelve hours when a couple of F-4 drones started overflying the mothballed ship. Two destroyers fired off a barrage of missiles to overfly at the same time.

Hanging at thirty kilometers altitude, Winchester pitched its nose almost straight down, General Frank looked over to Babs and Marco and said, "Let's see what you bad kids got."

Babs activated the G screen. Slowly she pushed the touch screen control and scrolled down to send a tight gradient G field screen from the Winchester at 2000 kilometers per hour toward the sea. She had programmed a stop at fifty meters above the sea. The drones and missiles twisted apart by the shearing energy of the gravity wave. Marco evenly spaced three punches from stem to stern from the grav focus rod onto the target ship. The mothballed destroyer shifted lower and lower in the water and rolled over ten minutes later. Gen. Frank looked very ominous. It was not at all apparent he was happy with what he had just witnessed. The Taiwanese looked relieved said, "You may well save my country from slavery. We will have a historical debt."

Oliver quickly replied "We prefer to have no publicity. People in high places know of course, but I don't want the general public to know at this time. Public opinion in politics is not our friend. Please find some other way to explain it."

"As you wish. The important people will keep quiet, but we will remember," Gen Chao then asked. "Can we return directly to Taipei?"

"Yes, that would be best. Al, call Ariel and tell her to bring the Dorney to Taipei. She can pick up Jed since he can help sack groceries."

"How wide is that screen Babs?" Admiral Smith asked.

"This close to the earth about 30 km. When we are in space, we can spread it out to a few hundred km. The gradient is not as tight though."

"Tight enough to twist up a tube made of 3-inch steel?" Admiral Smith asked as he held Gen. Frank's gaze.

"Yes, I think so."

"Even if it had a lot of internal bulkheads?"

"Maybe not like a wad of gum, but enough for it to lose structural integrity. And we are improving it constantly," she replied.

"Marco, same question with that focus rod," Admiral Smith continued.

"It would probably take more than one punch but yea it could penetrate. The focus is about the same here or out in space. Likewise, we are getting better. Admiral Smith, remember the new ship will have a much bigger focus rod."

"Who is Al and are you going to sack up satellites like groceries?" Gen. Frank asked.

"AI is the man behind the curtain, also one of the math wizards improving the tech. And yes Ariel, Gabriela and Jed will sack them up with mylar sheets. Where do you want your groceries delivered?" Oliver replied.

"Just collect them together for now. Eventually, the lunar base will be the more discrete place," Gen. Frank replied.

"General Chao we will need twenty meter by twenty-meter sheets of mylar for each satellite to be blinded," Oliver requested.

"You shall have them."

Arriving in Taipei, they found Jed and Ariel supervising the loading of rolled up mylar sheet.

"That was really fast. How did they get that much mylar cut up and to the airport so quickly?" Oliver asked.

Gen. Chao just smiled and said, "This is Taiwan, we make everything, and everything is close."

"Where is Gabriela?" Marco asked his wife.

"Hiding in the cockpit. She was worried of being seen since she is an active-duty Brazilian officer." Ariel snickered.

"I wasn't thinking. You all take care up there and use your lifelines. Those satellites might have some surprise defensive systems," Marco then gave Ariel a deep long kiss.

"God, I love combat," Ariel sighed, then perked up, "Remember last time we were in a really bloody fight?"

"Oh yea, and I remember right after the fight we got really, really nasty. Didn't even wait to wash off their blood."

"Ooomft, I think I just came a little," Babs joked or maybe not as she got an unfocused stare for a moment.

∞

The greatest air armada the modern world had ever seen, took off from all over mainland China. First came air superiority fighters, but their opponents stayed in deep hanger bunkers. Partially frustrated but feeling victorious, they called the fighter bombers in and the fleet also started the crossing at thirty knots. Tight behind the bombers were the airborne elite troops. The Strait of Taiwan was full of soldiers.

Satellite coverage started winking out. One every ten minutes went off the air. Other than this, there was no resistance. Maybe the Taiwanese would rollover instead of fight. When the concentration was deemed to be at a maximum, General Chao humbly asked the Battleship Aerospace Detachment of American Space Services to assist his country against the aggressors. History would eventually record that BADASS had helped win Taiwan's definitive independence.

With Al coordinating the targets, Winchester started its zigzag up the straits. In sixty minutes, nothing was left in the air or on the sea. Since the Chinese generals were blinded, they ordered the second wave. Everything in the air died. The ships had been able to get most of their people into life rafts. Finally, someone noticed the radar return from thirty kilometers altitude and started shooting missiles at Winchester. Babs took care of the missiles with her G screen but let the others know they had been spotted. This sort of devastation might be reason enough to toss a nuclear warhead at them. It was time to retreat. More than enough had already been accomplished.

Roswell Boneyard

"I didn't want to bring this up since we were so busy killing those Chinese people but one of my threads picked up a convoy like the one that went to your parent's ranch. They are going through Roswell right now," Al informed Babs.

"We still have guys working the boneyard there. We need to warn the QRF!" Babs said.

"Oh, I already talked with Jerry. He has everyone out and set up in an ambush."

"You did that while in the heat of battle?" Babs asked amazed.

"It wasn't that hot. I have good air conditioning down here. My personality did not have to get very involved during the targeting. That is more math coprocessor time. Jerry is a fun guy. He told me all the ways they are going to fuck them up. Even has some SAMs set up to take out their extraction force."

"Sucks to be them, I'll owe Jerry and LaShawn a good one. Marco and Ariel were talking about the after-battle party they had. It got me pulsing all over." Babs mulled it over for a second. "Let Jerry know I will come and debrief him afterward. LaShawn should attend too. Now I have to think how I will get to Roswell in the next few hours," Babs said.

"We could go up and you swap out with Ariel. Captain Queiroz could help with the debriefing," Al offered.

"Al you are a genius. We go up, I swap with Ariel and Winchester collects all the Chinese satellites. And Ariel is with her hubby," Babs said.

"You and your creation will take over the world one day Babs," Oliver cut in. "Let's go get some birds Number One."

General Chao called this command post on Q comm releasing his fighters and surface ships to clean up. The Empire lost seventy thousand soldiers and sailors in one afternoon. The elite troops who had been the backbone of power were all dead. More importantly, most of the dead were the only sons of their family. The retribution by the families on the known representatives of the Empire throughout the country was biblical. The new China Empire was crippled before its first year of the new dynasty. But they did hold to power.

∞

Captain Wang had assembled his men in an old oilfield man camp fifty miles east of Roswell just below the caprock. They had trickled in over the last week in a variety of vehicles. Today is the day he thought. China will have Taiwan and I will capture technology even better than Col. Wu. They would escape in military transport planes and fly directly to Mexico just like the Port Aransas raid.

Or not.

∞

Dorney settled down in the patio of the QRF. Organized chaos was all around. Troopers were frog marching prisoners wearing official PLA uniforms off to holding cells, some prisoners were being attended by medics and other soldiers were unloading gear from Piranha V infantry fight vehicles. One truck was squatting low piled with body bags. They all had stopped as Dorney descended.

Babs and Gabriela came stomping down the folding stairs. They had left Jed with the Winchester and the zippers of their flight suits down to their navels. Gabriela stood with her hands on her hips while the men gawked.

"Jerry, LaShawn it's time for the debrief," Babs shouted to the crowd.

The pair came hustling up still grimy from the recent firefight.

"Ready when you are ma'am."

"Get on board," Babs ordered.

Everyone boarded and Dorney shot to orbit.

"Babs, we got a call from Al in time to evacuate all the civilians. The Chinese trooper must have expected total surprise because their convoy was bunched up coming thru the base gate. We had set up a classic L shape ambush with armor support. They didn't stand a chance. A few of your hangers have some extra ventilation now, sorry."

"Nothing less than I expected. But that is not the kind of debrief we were expecting. Take off your briefs." Babs said as she disengaged the floor gravity going to zero G. She and Gabriela pulled their flight suits the rest of the way off exposing four of the most perfect breasts ever enhanced by zero G.

"Oh, ooh!!" Jerry and LaShawn said in unison as they debriefed.

Babs grabbed the first handle that floated by squeezing it."

"Babs, I have some results from the speed run experiment." Al's voice came over the speaker.

"I'm gonna unplug you when I get back." Babs shrieked.

"It can wait til later then," Al said.

Babs was sure he was snickering whichever way a computer could snicker. She gave her handle another tug to bring herself in close.

Sorting it out

Cida had assumed the role of head of hotel services for the lunar base. She was making it comfortable for everyone. They now had forty quarters operating, twenty with couples and the rest housing sixty other people. She shared her quarters with Babs and Gabriela when they were around. The kitchens were producing four quality meals a day and one snack laid out between each. The logistics were demanding but Al had taught her to use spreadsheets and he kept a virtual eye out for problems. Occasionally when she had a spare moment, she thought back to her life of little more than a year ago. Her life now was not something she was able to even imagine then.

"Hey Al?"

"Yes Cida?"

"How is my horse Carlo doing?"

"He is fit and in good health. I think he likes working cattle with the other horses," Al responded. "He is in the barn now would you like to see him?"

"You can do that?"

"Yes, we have recently installed many cameras around the ranch. Marco is afraid of revenge raids from the Chinese." And Carlo appeared via hologram 3D in Cida's quarters. The sudden appearance made her jump a little.

"You are appearing in front of him on a hologram as well. He can hear your voice," Al told her.

Cida started speaking to him and Carlo responded, bouncing his head and nickering.

"Oh Carlo, I wish I could give you a good brushing," Cida said and suddenly everything felt right in her world. After all, she planned to go back for a few days next week. A few minutes later she got a comm from Oliver to come to the conference room for a crew meeting.

∞

"So, Al now that we have the crew together, tell us about the speed run," Babs said as the group sat in the conference room.

"You won't unplug me?"

"You know better. So, what sort of mischief did you get into by yourself?"

"Well, here is a video of the pass at the maximum speed we reach during a regular run to the belt going through pea gravel and dust in slow motion?" Al used the 3D hologram.

They watched as the barge arrived frame by frame and a fireworks display lit up showing the bubble volume.

"The next is at the same speed but with fist sized to basketball sized," Al continued.

It appeared the same, but the fireworks were blindingly bright, some frames washing out the camera.

"Any inertia leakage, radiation or temperature spikes?" Dr. Lee asked.

"None within the accuracy of the instruments," Al said and continued. "I hit something of relatively the same mass as the barge at these same speeds and it had the same effect. This time the cameras washed out completely. Almost no debris was thrown in any iteration. Even the biggest asteroid just came apart. By the way, that biggest one was full of metal, mostly nickel-iron. All of the material expended itself in light, particle energy and heat."

"This is all great news. How did you finally destroy the lamb?" Dr. Lee asked.

"Well, Jed made a comment about relativistic speed, so I backed up to Neptune and started from there."

"I don't suppose you picked up any solid nitrogen?" Oliver asked.

"Did you want some?"

"It would have been convenient for the lunar base but go ahead."

"So, I accelerated at twenty-five Gs," Al said, 'Jesus' someone else muttered, "I passed through the fist sized rocks at point one light speed. Easy peasy. But, big but, I was thinking about how cool that was and crunching some numbers and almost missed my turn around Jupiter. Would have been going interstellar if it were a smaller planet. G drive loses a lot of traction out in the outer system. Gotta be careful."

"That actually was a good adventure."

"Sure was. Let's do it again sometime. Really, I quite enjoyed myself. Where do you want your solid nitrogen?"

"You did pick some up, great. That stuff must be really cold, where is it now?" Oliver asked.

"In the shadow of the moon, there are about twenty tons now, but it is sublimating. You are going to lose about a ton a month. The barge is holding it suspended half a meter above the deck."

"Before I start making useless orders have you made any arrangements?" Oliver asked.

"Nothing that cannot be canceled. Embraer designed some special valves for their airlocks. I have a good, used oilfield gas centrifuge boxed for shipment."

"Ariel, can you set up a plan to have a chamber to let the nitrogen ice sublimate and run through the gas separator?" Oliver said, "Al, any idea as to the purity and other gases present?"

"I hit it with the spectroscopy laser and there is about five percent mix of hydrogen, helium and methane. The gas separator I ordered is set up for this mix. No suspended solids."

"Excellent. Let's just vent the rest. Anyone have a calculator to figure out how much space we can fill at ten psi?" Babs said.

"You wound me. It will fill all the opened and dressed tunnels to eleven psi." Al said.

"Just me messing with you."

"I said I was sorry about that Dorney interruption," Al didn't sound contrite, "So get everything moving?"

"Yes, it will be nice not to have a bunch of runs just for atmosphere," Oliver said. "Your work just increased the team's productivity. We have been holding ourselves down to five Gs. I think we can bump up to ten Gs. I still want more time with our tech to feel comfortable at Gs that would squash us."

"Yeah, besides we are not in that big of a hurry," Interjected Marco.

"Ariel, how is manufacturing?" Oliver asked.

"We have completed the cells for the Nautilus. We are halfway through a set for another Winchester type craft. Have not started on more floor panels. If we are going to get serious about manufacturing for Telemark, we need to rethink our processes in both execution and scale. It is time to source some industrial automation professionals. Oliver, you have been dealing with Mr. Abril. They are probably going to need something similar to keep up with the graphene sheet production," she replied.

"And we are talking about a lot more people. I think we are to the stage of getting a human resources manager," Oliver said and everybody groaned.

"We will keep them pitifully weak if that makes you feel better," Oliver said taking a deep breath, "And the Nautilus. Gen Frank said they are ready to deliver. That is a very big chunk of iron. I want to propose we, the crew, install just enough cells to get it into lunar orbit. After it is up here, we can use base personnel to help finish it."

That brought a murmur of approval. Everyone was already overworked.

"Don't we own that semi-sub?" Marco asked.

"We do," Oliver affirmed.

"We don't have to worry about secrecy anymore since the Taiwan slap down. Couldn't the Navy do the work in San Diego for any future sub conversion? We could bring the semi-sub to orbit to act as a shipyard. It has a near perfect geometry."

"Wow, that is a great idea," Oliver said. "Mr. Abril also indicated true zero G could be used in some of his processes."

"And biologicals, crystals, and other things I don't know about," Ariel said. "The semi-sub could put together a long cylinder when it isn't working on ships. Workers could live in a G environment and commute over to work in the cylinder. Or Rectangle."

"The semi-sub may be the perfect setup to bring in NewOrigins. Elton has been quiet, but I know he is thinking now is the time for both cells in a Telemark and NewOrigins space contracting. We need to give some back to the USA. The Space Force has been very good to us," Oliver said. "And we have one and a half billion dollars in the bank."

There was a momentary silence.

"You were going to tell us this when?" Dr. Lee finally decided to contribute.

"Anybody want to cash out?" Oliver asked and everyone shook their heads. "How about a big steak and lobster party for the whole base? Beer, fine wine, and whiskey til we puke." That led to a small cheer.

"Cida that is going to be on you to arrange."

"I can do a lot with half a billion dollars," Cida said which brought a small laugh.

"Another item is greens and vegetables. We should get a start on this project as well. Cida are you interested or should we look for a horticulture specialist?" Oliver asked.

"I've had enough of growing big vegetable gardens, but I would like a small area to grow some for myself."

"My thinking was some scientific hydroponic installation Maybe we should go to the effort to have a place to get our hands in the dirt. Living in a cave distances us from the natural world," Oliver said.

"I don't have much of a green thumb, but it would be nice to help in someone else's garden." Dr. Lee said.

"If we have a larger population, we will still need the hydroponics I think," Marco added.

"Al, how is your new home extension coming along?"

"Bought and in a box. I would rather it was installed after the Nautilus is in orbit. Too many greasy fingers on Earth. There will be two new systems for the Winchester and next craft. I will set up a non-sentient A.I. for each," Al replied.

"Great and I feel ya. Bring it up on the Dorney?"

"Yes, please."

"Lots to do folks. We are scheduled to be in Kwajalein in three days."

After the meeting, Oliver pulled Ariel aside.

"Is chasing that mineral vein having any results?" he asked her.

"Yes. Next meeting, I will bring it up. I stopped Pedro and Michael from going further. There is brine mixing in with the rock. Some gold and copper are also showing up. The temperature is already at twenty-two degrees. We should get a mining engineer involved."

'We are in luck. I went to New Mexico Institute of Mining and Technology. Some of my friends are miners. It is good that you stopped. We don't want to flood the tunnels. Maybe even set a safety door just in case."

"Will do."

Orbiting drill rigs

"Elton, we would like a meeting in Kwajalein next week. There is a good opportunity for NewOrigins I would like to show you," Oliver said.

"I'll clear my calendar. Can you pick me up in Austin?"

"Yes, I will send Gabriela in the Dorney. Coordinate with her, she can pick you up most anywhere discrete. We are past the secrecy phase, but I still don't want us on the tabloids."

"Understood, see you there."

Oliver's next call was to Gen. Frank.

"We want to have a meeting at Kwajalein next week when we are installing the cells on the Nautilus, care to join us, maybe bring Adm. Smith?"

"Love too but I have some bad news. I heard it on the grapevine that President Cruz was going to fire me and maybe prosecute," Gen. Frank said.

"I know this must be about us and Taiwan. His cabal of corporations must have lost enormously on China being brought low."

"They did. I can make Kwajalein but doubt I have more than a month of being effective."

"We may be able to help. I know a guy who knows a guy," Oliver joked.

"Yeah, I got a call from a concerned citizen once. Probably the same guy."

"Probably. I'll have Gabriela pick you up. See you next week."

"Right, see you."

After Gen. Frank disconnected, Oliver sat a few moments thinking.

"Al, do you have a recording of that conversation between President Cruz and Emperor Peng that would stand up to the court of public opinion?"

"Yes, and I have some follow up conversations of the underlings who were tasked to accomplish their agreement."

"We need a leak by a high government official and a media campaign. Time for traitors to get their due," Oliver said with iron in his voice.

"Elton has the best media people, but I have a nice package for downing the traitors. I have identified whistleblowers and news outlets ideal to make it happen. Should I pull the trigger?" Al asked anxiously.

"Bloodthirsty today, are we? No time like the present. This is overdue anyway. Go."

∞

By the time they got to Kwajalein, a veritable political shit storm was blowing. As they eased Winchester full of grav drive cells onto the helideck, Gen. Frank, Adm. Smith and Elton Mark were standing at the access door grinning like possums. As the crew walked down the cargo ramp, Gen. Frank couldn't contain himself anymore.

"Yea, I know a guy," He shouted. His professional life had been saved and he was extremely grateful.

"Let's go inside and get some business out of the way. We have a lot of physical work to do but I want to get through initial agreements while we are fresh."

"Where are Dr. Lee and Jed?" Elton asked.

"The stayed on the lunar base. They are hatching something bigger than grav drive. But don't ask any questions and I'll tell you no lies," Oliver shut down the conversation before it started.

∞

Jed and Merry Lee were looking over a kludged together package the size of a small car.

"We better take this to the surface to try it," Jed stated.

"Oh yeah," Dr. Lee agreed. "If this works, we will have all the fuel Earth will need right here on the moon. This is one of the best places to harvest helium-3 in all the solar system. That's worth more than all the gold or diamonds. Real practical energy for all."

"Yea, yea, let's go?"

"Let's."

They decided to take it to the bottom of a steep crater and monitor from inside a Telemark pickup in a crater nearby.

"Ok, initial volume of helium-3 and deuterium are in place, compress it."

A grav bubble compressed down the volume as more mixture was injected in behind. The second bubble compressed the second volume as the first bubble was switched off. In this manner, they pumped up to a critical mass and the mixture ignited. The last bubble merely contained the reaction. Enormous quantities of heat were being created. The absorption was in a lattice of circulating sodium. The sodium was going through a heat exchanger buried in the regolith. All was going well. They had not injected any more fuel after ignition. While they were busy congratulating themselves, the regolith started melting.

"Oh shit," Jed said, "eject the core, eject the core!"

Dr. Lee's fingers flew across the keyboard. They watched the monitors as the beachball sized core of grav cells flew straight up from their device. At two hundred meters a tiny sun was born and died.

"Well, we know it works now. Just need a bigger heat exchanger," Dr. Lee said. "This changes everything, again."

'Hey Al, you around?" Jed called.

"Yes, and congratulations."

"You too. You helped get this together," Jed said. "Let Oliver know it worked. The subs are good, but the fission reactor won't be needed anymore."

"I'll let him know. We gonna go SOOO fast."

∞

"We are ready to take possession of the Nautilus. There will be a little change up though. We will also be taking the semi-sub into orbit," Oliver said. This caused the military group to sit back in their chairs. Only Gen. Frank and Adm. Smith understood.

"That was you over the Straits of Taiwan?" a captain asked.

"Yes, aren't you glad we are on your side?" Marco interjected. The military men nodded their heads.

"Since that event, we feel it is no longer necessary to carry on with secrecy. The next refurb can take place easily in a dry dock in San Diego, correct Adm. Smith?"

"Yes, but the question is, whose sub will it be?" Smith replied.

"Good question, like your reactor, our grav drive cells will not be sold, only leased, nor will I share the technology for the screens and focus rods. Lasers, rail guns and missiles will dominate any other opponent. But leave the propeller shaft in place. The world is an uncertain place," Oliver said a little nervous of the reaction. One of the Navy captains was getting red in the face.

"Before you say anything, Chester," Gen. Frank said addressing the red-faced man, "This will be a Space Force show and it is acceptable to me. They are right to be nervous about unleashing this weapon. It crushed the Chinese with no loss to the Space Force. The rest of the world would be terrified of us. Frightened people and nations make bad decisions."

Chester's face relaxed as he saw the wisdom of that statement. Oliver and his crew gave a small sigh of relief as well.

"Now what in tarnation will you do with a semi-sub in space?" Col. Rankin of the USMC asked.

"Why, train Marines of course," Cap. Chester responded regaining his humor.

"Training Marines for zero G combat actually is not a bad idea. We will make room for you," Oliver said, "Mainly, we are going to build things. It has the right geometry and already has industrial spaces. Eventually ships will need repair. It is not so far-fetched as it sounds, except for lifting it up there. When we fly the Nautilus out from the lagoon, you will understand."

"And NewOrigins?" Elton queried.

"I am hoping NewOrigins will operate it. My crew is up to its eyeballs in other work and your depth and industrial knowledge fits. I would like for you to take Embraer on as a junior partner. This really needs to turn into a global concern. We can talk about applying a lower level of this tech to your Telemarks, but that can be done afterward just between us."

"Don't forget Mars," Ariel prompted.

"Right, we want to start a truly international campaign to colonize Mars. I expect NewOrigins to lead the first base there since they have been working on tech to make it happen. Later people and companies of other nations will get a chance to make it work for themselves. There is an enormous **BUT**. All political affiliations with Earth must be left on Earth. I don't want Liechtenstein carving out territory and calling it New Liechtenstein. The charter will be drawn up during a conference at our lunar base with restricted communications with the shadow bosses. Neither big corporations nor big countries will dominate this, or the deal is off. This is not, repeat not, a United Nations thing," Oliver laid out.

Everyone chuckled. "You don't have to convince us. A media campaign will be essential to keep the restless masses docile. The mobs will lose their minds about this," Col. Rankin said.

Oliver thinking to himself *'And I didn't even mention nuclear fusion'.*

∞

The physical work to get the cells into the slots along the hull was taxing even with the reduced work plan. Three fourths of the way through, they decided to lift with what they had and finish the rest in zero gravity. Elton had assembled a camera crew. With the crew dressed in white lining the top deck, they made a classic swing around the lagoon with half the hull submerged. The people knew what they had been transforming scrap into now, but it was nice to watch it sail out to sea.

 Rumors and conspiracy theories were already swirling in the press about the mystery plane that helped free Taiwan. It was time to control the narrative. Elton's media team had already outlined the campaign which was first going to be the great journey to Mars. They decided that the Winchester would be best. It was big enough and could land directly on the surface. There would be a good photo op of the Telemark pickup truck rolling out onto the surface to claim a new world for offroaders everywhere.

If a major portion of the truth reached the world press without control, every sort of opinion would virtually explode into the world's psyche. Before the announcement, Ariel and Marco convinced their parents to come spend some time on the lunar base, far from lunatics and assassins. This was going to be a time of danger.

Right after the Nautilus lifted, NewOrigins crews went to work on the semi-sub sealing vents welding hatches and generally readying it for a space environment. Slots were welded in for grav cells in the pontoons. Insulation and CO_2 capture were installed, ventilation systems reworked. Plumbing setup had to be able to turn off during zero G times because shit flowing downhill still needs a hill. New machine tools were installed, and old oilfield systems were completely stripped out. Extra decks were built over the areas once used for drill pipe storage. Cranes removed their booms and laid them aside for future needs to berth ships under construction. The semi-sub would need three months to be ready for lifting.

Shotgun

"Ma, Pa, the trip to Mars will take less than a week. We will do a bunch of silly stunts, record even more non-sense and then be back. Normally Cida would be around to take care of you, but we want to include her in this historic moment. If it weren't for us fighting for Taiwan, we would have had more time to ease into this. As you might imagine, the world will go a little crazy about this for a while. You already saw what insanity can happen not so long ago."

"We understand Ariel. It will be a hoot. At least for a couple of weeks. Do you think we can stay with Marco's parents on your ranch in Brazil after?" Lyle asked.

"Absolutely, but let's play it by ear. No tellin' how long it will take for the dust to settle," Ariel said.

"I liked it there the other times we visited. A nice rustic atmosphere and they work cattle on horseback. We fit right in," Martha said and pointing at the Dorney, "Now we have to go to the moon in that jalopy?"

"Don't worry ma I'll drive."

"Can I sit upfront?" Martha asked.

"Hey," Lyle complained.

"She called shotgun Pa."

∞

"Mom please be reasonable. It will be very dangerous for you even in Paris for the next few months. The Pettigrews already had a kidnap attempt. After we make this announcement tomorrow, all hell is going to break loose," Marco pleaded with his mother. "The Pettigrews and dad are already up there."

"You said it was very rough. I will have to wear big shoes. That simply won't do," Marli Rocha sniffed.

"Let's make a deal, I bet one of your famous chefs would do anything to get to go to the moon and do a cooking show for a few weeks. They can owe you that favor," Marcos proposed and shut up because he could see by his mother's face, he had already sold the deal.

"They will need many costly ingredients. And fine wine of course."

Marcos grinned because he essentially had an unlimited budget for such things. Especially if the lunar personnel would benefit from fine dining for a period. Great food is the best way to keep up morale in a confined workforce. The publicity would help recruiting in later years.

"Done," Marco offered his hand.

"Done," his mother said and shook on it. "Oh my, I think I settled too low."

"Here, this would have been the rest of the bribe mother," Marco said and took out a platinum necklace with a five-caret blue diamond pendant and placed it around her neck.

"Oh son, that is one of those diamonds all the truly wealthy women have been flaunting in my face," Marli said admiring the stone.

"My crew have been harvesting those stones in the asteroid belt. I picked that one with my own hands," Marco confided to his mother. "Let's go, Ariel is waiting on the roof."

Marli was weeping a little, "My Marco, my Marco you are going to be the richest man in the world."

"Only one of the richest. Really we need to leave."

"Whatever you say, dear," Marli said totally compliant now.

∞

The camera crews had been working overtime getting footage of the Winchester, Dorney and Nautilus from inside and out. They were not allowed to video much of the base, just the kitchens and living quarters. It was none of the world's business as far as Oliver was concerned. Mars was plenty big enough of a show.

"Whenever you are ready Mr. Mark we are recording," the cameraman said.

Elton Mark was sitting in the Hanger overlook with the Winchester below and the moonscape beyond it.

"Fellow Earthlings," he laughed. "I always wanted to say that. We are ready to embarque on the next great chapter in human history. Tomorrow the Winchester will take a team to Mars for the first time. We will leave a block of supplies there two days from now. Supplies that will be used by the first colonists. Those colonists will be there in two months. Those times are actual.

A small company has developed revolutionary technology that enables this marvel. NewOrigins will lead the way with the first phase, but soon opportunities will be open to the whole world.

There is a catch. A conference will be held here on the moon in three months' time to develop a charter for future social organization on Mars. One thing has been made clear, Earth politics will remain on Earth. This is a new beginning, not a continuation of the past. We will have a Mars landing video soon. Now enjoy a tour of these marvelous machines and a little of the lunar base," Elton swiveled in his chair to look at the lunar landscape.

"Short and sweet boss. The compilation of the rest is already done. When do you want it to go to Austin? You know something like this will leak like a sieve."

"Get it on the air about four pm on the east coast. Europe will still be awake." Elton replied.

"Come on, let's go rock the world," The cameraman said as the assistant packed up.

∞

To say that the world howled upon seeing the ASS Spacecraft and lunar base was an understatement. So much social media was created it "broke" the internet. Most of the individuals wanted to go or find out how they could get a job. All the talking heads, who are mouthpieces for large organizations, were saying essentially, how dare you do something without us or our blessing. China recognized the Winchester but did not say anything. Their revenge would have to wait.

This was the final straw for President Cruz. Congress started impeachment proceedings when they realized what he was trying to give away to our enemies. But he was not without teeth and once again the FBI raided the Roswell Boneyard. Their attitude was different this time.

A polite knock was answered by the same scruffy janitor. "Oh, hi guys, come on in, we've been expecting you."

"Hi, we are with the FBI and have a search warrant for these premises," a senior agent said politely.

"Sure, sure. What are you searching for? I might be able to help you find it."

We have a warrant for all computers, spacecraft, and devices used with the same," the agent said.

"All that stuff is at our lunar base. Do you need the address?" scruffy said.

The agents just had wry smiles at the smartass comment. "Guess we will poke around a little then let the Attorney General know. Maybe he will buy us passage to go there."

"Hey boss, I'll volunteer to go," said the youngest member of the team.

"I got seniority, kiddo," the senior agent replied to his underling. Turning back to the janitor, "thanks for your time sir, we'll be on our way now." And with that, the FBI team went away.

Mars

"There is the Curiosity over there. Looks like we are in its camera angle. Babs, you told JPL we were going to be here?" Oliver asked.

"Yea, they want us to wipe down the solar panels and clean the lens. The shift leader said he would turn on the continuous video mode for our venture out," Babs replied. "You ready Elton?"

"Oh baby, I've been looking for this my whole life. I expected it to be some steely eyed astronauts doing the first step though," Elton said. "Remember folks our radios will be live so take a little care what you say. Al will be doing a five sec delay, but he may not filter everything."

They dropped landing gear and sat down about a hundred meters in front of the Mars rover Curiosity with the cargo ramp facing it. Cida and Elton, holding hands, were the first to step off. Everyone thought it was both ironic and fitting. The rest of the crew sort of swarmed out in no order. The cameraman had a hard time keeping up since he was unused to spacesuits and reduced gravity. Gabriela was playing as his assistant today.

"Al, can you get the JPL shift leader on the radio?" Oliver asked.

"Just a minute," Al replied.

"JBL Control Center this is John."

"Hi John, this is Oliver Eversole. I'm looking at Curiosity. Is there anything else you would like us to do maintenance wise while we are here? Babs is cleaning the solar panels and will do the lenses next. We are assuming alcohol is ok for the lens."

"Is this a joke, Oliver Eversole is on Mars right now. I just watched him come off his spaceplane." John said indignantly.

"Look at the TV again John," Oliver said and started waving back at the ship.

"This whole thing is a hoax?"

"You will see our boot prints through a clean lens. We have real-time communications, no time lag, which by the way you should keep to yourself for the time being," Oliver replied knowing the guy was not believing just yet. "We call it Q comm and we can hang a set on your buggy if you like. It will save a lot of power and you can drive Curiosity around in real-time. So, you want one or not?"

"Uhm, yes please?" John still in a state of disbelief. There is a connector just under the radio box for data."

"Yea, Babs has already talked to some of your techs. I wanted to get permission before messing with your stuff. The Q comm is already packaged up for you. Just a minute," When Oliver gave her the thumbs up, Babs swapped out the radio connection.

"Ok John, you should be seeing live now."

"Oh my god," was all John could say.

"So, you want to swap out batteries or anything?" Oliver asked again.

"No, the batteries are holding strong. With no radio to push and clean solar panels, it's better than new."

"Ok then we are going to go screw around with the truck and take some selfies. Later John," Oliver said.

"Later"

Oliver started walking about fifty meters behind Babs toward the Winchester. She reached it first and jumped in the truck with Elton. Over the radio she said, "Hey Oliver we are going to drive up to the top of that ridge and take in the view."

"Ok, we are going to set up a seismic station the folks at NASA sent with us," Oliver replied. "It will take a couple of hours or so since we need to dig a hole for the seismometer."

∞

"Cida, switch it on here," Jed pointed to the power button. "I have programmed them to have less torque because of the lower gravity. Careful when you go over a rise because you can catch some serious air."

Jed and Cida rode their electric cycles down the cargo ramp out onto the Mars plain. They rode off about a hundred yards and stopped. Jed then burned a couple of donuts raising a dust cloud. Then they circled around so they could ride straight through it looking totally gnarly like the camera man asked for. Everyone was having a super fun time. Through digging the hole for Dr. Lee's seismometer, Marco rode a wheelie down the cargo ramp and proceeded to use every bump to catch air on his electric cycle. After mounting the seismic station solar panels, Gabriela and Ariel brought out the grav cycles and proceed to show the kids what gnarly really meant. It was fun but it was also a practical checkout of some equipment meant for the Mars colony.

"Hey, what are Babs and Elton up to? They have been sitting on that ridge for like an hour," Dr. Lee asked as he tried to knock the Mars dust off from digging in the seismometer.

"If I know Babs, she is breaking in a new planet and Elton is getting what he deserves for his dedication to bringing humanity to Mars," Ariel replied. "Oh crap, Al delete that last."

Thirty seconds later Al responded, "Delete what?"

The next day's banner headline of the Daily Mail read *'Babs breaks in Red Planet'* and below in smaller print *'Elton Mark finally gets his just reward.'*

The sun was getting low and everyone was running out of gas. Oxygen too. Time to head for home. They lowered the container with habitation tents onto the open plain and stowed the cycles inside. Elton decided he wanted the truck to go back to Earth for the Smithsonian. It was driven back up the ramp. The crew lifted for Earth orbit soon after.

The people of Earth were stunned at the turn of history. And the way it was turned. No steely eyed astronauts trying to look brave. Just a bunch of young people out for a lark. Some even got laid. What a day.

Nautilus

It was a working shakedown cruise for the Nautilus. The propeller shaft was working as a gravity focus rod above and beyond all expectations. The inside of the bubble acted as an anvil. The two together were like a giant eating peanuts on a chunk of asteroid. In one hour, a twenty-meter diameter boulder was reduced to fist sized gravel. Ariel and Babs, piloting two grav cycles with grav screen pods on temporary mounts, herded the debris into one of the missile canister hatches left in place from the sub's refit. Babs asked Al to close and lock the hatch.

Babs and Ariel backed their cycles one after the other through one of the old missile canister's hatches with small thrusters. It opened into a space that had previously been where there were four missile canisters. The grav cycles latched into brackets beside each other. There was plenty of clearance for the girls in EV suits to get to the airlock built into the bottom. Not long after, they had peeled out of the used NewOrigins spacesuits and stored them in the lockers beside the airlock.

Ariel said, "We need to think about setting this space up as a proper ready room. You know like have common tools, parts, and guns to go with the lockers."

"Don't know about the guns but yeah, I feel ya."

Not long after, they were sitting in the mess eating green chili cheeseburgers chasing them with ice cold beer.

"Nice work out there. You two would make good cowgirls, rounding up them doggies," Marty cracked as he and Jed came into the mess. Marty had just come off second shift on the bridge, "Marcos and Oliver have the smelter going but it will be a couple of days before we can load more rock."

"I know you were being funny, but Babs and I actually worked cattle on horseback. We really are cowgirls," Ariel said, "My Dad has a ranch over in the Red River Valley northeast of Lubbock."

"So, what do you think of the grav cycles as quarter horses?" Jed asked.

"Weird, it's kind of the same keeping the rocks together, but using joysticks and virtual gloves on a cycle where a horse would be jumping around is something else entirely," Ariel explained.

"I really like it. Feels as though you are flowing in a ballet," Babs added.

Mimi, Gary and David came into the mess drawn by the smell of cheeseburgers. They would be going on shift in about an hour.

"How come your suit liners look so good? I look like lumpy laundry in mine," Mimi asked addressing Ariel.

"Ma taught me how to sew and we need them to fit snug. If it doesn't, you get a lot of chaffing after a few hours in vacuum in all the wrong places. And it's hard to scratch out there," Ariel responded.

"All I got was safety training. Heard you say it was fun breaking rocks. Maybe I could cross-train. Running a reactor is what I know, but really working in zero G is my life fantasy."

"Everyone should be getting cross training out here. It's not like we can call the temp worker agency," Ariel said. "I'd be happy to take you out and get you started."

Mimi was thrilled. Real space work.

∞

"It's going to be a couple of days to digest the last load so let's survey toward Ceres checking for density along the way. We can break them down between ice, carbonate and metal," Oliver said.

"OK, we will go slow enough to get good orbital values for each, that way we can find them again more easily," Babs replied.

"We have a database for the bigger ones. Let's zigzag between those and catalog the smaller stuff referenced to the bigger asteroids. I want to check out Ceres anyway. Maybe a good place to establish a base like we have on the moon."

"I want a swimming pool and beach this time with a light big enough it looks like the sun," Babs demanded.

"We can probably make that happen," Oliver said which put a smile on her face.

Ceres

"We have a good radar/lidar map. Let's go check out that gouge. What did this, a sideswipe of a big asteroid or comet?" Oliver pondered.

It became increasingly obvious the cave entrance on Ceres was not natural. After twenty meters the wall became a regular rectangle. After thirty meters there were material coatings. At fifty meters they encountered an airlock. Everyone had been silent as they walked down the ramp. Oliver was the first to speak.

"Well, at least they seem to have been about our size."

"Whoever they are," Jed said.

"Hey, there is a mechanical override, shall we?" Marco asked.

"Hell yeah, let's go explore the creepy space tunnel with alien ghosts," Babs whined.

"Stand back. If there is atmosphere, it'll blow who knows what out," Marco said as he laid into turning the crank. After he had cranked for a couple of minutes, the door was open enough to pass. The inner door was already open and the inside was in vacuum. Quickly, it became evident the previous occupants had taken basically everything leaving bare walls. No machinery or objects, just empty space. A mystery, but convenient for the company's needs.

"So now the question is, will it hold pressure?" Ariel said looking around.

"I was not seeing any rock fractures, so probably yes. The air had a long time to seep out even with the best seals," Oliver replied.

"So, how are we going to get enough atmosphere to fill this place?" Ariel asked always the practical one.

"Oxygen and carbon dioxide are easy enough, but eighty percent is nitrogen. First place that pops into my mind is Triton, Neptune's moon. A long way out, but maybe that is the best way since it is solid nitrogen. Maybe send a barge out again? For now, we can close off all but a small part and manage most gases from Earth. It's old, but humans would have been civilized at that time. I wonder if they had interactions with us?" Oliver thought out loud.

In their part of the search pattern, Marco and Ariel found another closed airlock. Looking through the small porthole the tunnel was completely filled with rock debris on the other side.

"Where are we in relation to the gouge, must be close?" Ariel puzzled.

"I figure about twenty or thirty meters. Maybe one of the grav cycles can dig this out." Marco said. "Rabbits always need more than one way out of their hole."

"The layout seems quadra-linear let's see if we can find more like this," Ariel suggested.

After three hours everyone met back at the entry. Dorney lifted them up to the Nautilus orbiting close above Ceres. They gathered in the conference room to download their individual routes with helmet cam footage.

"It looks like whatever made the gouge, took out a portion of the complex. Even so, what's left is very large. We could block off corridors here and here," Oliver pointed in the hologram. "That would give us living and working space and would not be too hard to fill with atmosphere."

"With this low gravity, a cradle to hold the Nautilus would be easy and truly make Ceres a full up support base," Ariel added.

"These are all good ideas, but I think we need to bring in General Frank right away. The mere existence of a complex here a thousand year old brings up solar system security questions. That really is why Space Force exists. Let's give him a call right now," Marco said.

"I think it's after midnight back home," Oliver pointed out.

"That is the fun part," Jed said and everyone got a good laugh.

"Do you know what time it is you bunch of nimrods?" Gen. Frank growled.

"And good morning to you too. I thought you should be our first call from our new base. Someone hollowed out a nice space for us on Ceres," Oliver said.

"What?" Gen Frank shouted and all could see him on the hologram jump straight to his feet, junk flapping. This caused intermittent snickering.

"No joke, someone or thing had a base here a thousand or two years ago."

"Don't touch anything! Can you get me and a team out there? Where is the Winchester?" the general was practically hyperventilating.

"You are in luck. They just finished a supply run to your moon base and are tucked away at our base. They could be wherever you need tomorrow, if you want to move that fast. I don't think you need a security force along. This place looks to have been abandoned a very long time. No machinery, but they did leave the wiring and control lines. Looks like copper for power and fiber for control. Not far off what we would use today," Oliver informed him. "by the way, your junk is still bouncing from that jump out of bed."

"Who cares? Who are the pilots of the Winchester? Can you get them headed my way?"

"That would be Gabriela and Alice. Yes, I will call them right after this. Will you be heavily loaded with personnel and gear?" Oliver inquired.

"No just a small team to evaluate and plan a bigger campaign," he replied.

"Then fill the rest of the space with bottles of liquid nitrogen. We can start turning this archeologic dig into a useful place. By the way, this place ultimately belongs to American Space Service."

"Yes, of course. It is only information for the Space Force I want right now. Space Force use of the base is to be negotiated if there is even a need for it."

∞

"Queiroz. Se sabe o que horas sao?" Gabriela said still mostly asleep.

"I heard hours in there, so I assume you are complaining about the time," Babs said.

"Babs, what's up? I thought you all were at the belt, mining."

"We were until we found an alien base dug into Ceres."

"What!" Gabriela shouted now fully awake jumping to her feet.

"Yea, the little green men pointed lasers at us and asked what we wanted," Babs carried on not letting her know the hologram was on in a conference call and she was only in panties in front of them.

"You did not wake me up just to fuck with me."

"The green men weren't there but someone or thing dug out a real nice base on Ceres. Need you to bring Gen. Frank out on the Winchester along with some eggheads. He will want you to pick him up ASAP. Al will coordinate with supplies."

"Wow, you really did find an alien base in our system?" Gabriela asked her eyes big.

"We really did, and it is sized just right for us. Need you to stuff as many bottles of liquid nitrogen as you can onboard. We can make oxygen here. See if Cida is up to a trip. She can see if any of this place would work for growing things," Ariel picked up the conversation. "By the way, you are in full color on our conference room hologram."

"Who cares. This is stupendous news."

Or Monsters

"I never thought those archeologists would leave. They didn't even come to any clear conclusions except to say that the lump of mummified material was probably a cat. Let's go grab that ice asteroid, tuck it into the gouge and head for home," Ariel said.

"This has been the longest trip we have ever made. Definitively beach time is called for. Right after a pig out in Sao Paulo," Babs declared.

"Give me the coordinates Al, I'll lay them in," Ariel said. "The one that's three thousand km in the trailing orbit."

The ice was very quickly located, and they were approaching to drag it along outside. Ceres was still very close.

"Hey, I am getting a sudden uptick in particle radiation," Jed informed the crew. "It looks kind of strange. I am going to run the magnetic field up to maximum just in case."

"Just in case of what?" Oliver asked.

"I don't know and that is the point."

"Good point, crank it up my man," Babs said.

"Hey! The ice roid just disappeared. It was right there," Babs said looking at the hologram feed. "The stars are different."

"Um, care to elaborate?" Oliver said as he moved to get a better look.

"Here is a quick playback. About the time Jed cranked up the Mag field, the stars simply changed. As in not the same stars in the same place. Look, there is a kind of fuzzy ring."

Roswell Boneyard

As the Nautilus shifted along its course the new stars changed perspective. It was as though they were looking through a window to another place. Then a red dwarf star came into view.

"Hey Toto, that is definitely not Kansas over there," Marco exclaimed in a loud voice.

"Settle down Dorothy, Jed try turning the Mag field back to where it was," Ariel suggested.

They watched as the stars returned to normal and the ice roid reappeared behind where the phenomenon was.

"Event horizon," Jed said.

"See if you can reactivate it," Oliver said.

It reappeared at 80% of full field. Jed cranked it off and on a couple of more times.

"Stable for here and now. Wonder if it stays put," Jed mumbled.

"I bet that is why the Ceres mystery base is where it is," Ariel suggested. "Makes sense from a logistical point of view, if this is a passageway. Maybe like a customs station. Question is, what is on the other side?"

"Marco, Babs let's go rig up a hover pallet as a probe with some Q Comm, cameras and whatever else comes to hand. After we shove it over there I want to see if the Q comm still works when the portal shuts off. Set up the camera to first record the local starfield. Let's find out where the other side is. Then if we are lucky, we can fly the probe around inside that system. Maybe we will find E.T.," Oliver said excitedly.

"Or monsters." Jeb sub-vocalized.

Roswell Boneyard

The ice roid drifted away completely ignored.

Thank you for reading the first book of a new series. _Please_, leave a review on Amazon so others can find this book.

About the Author

I have always lived my life out where the dogs bark. Whether it is hiking, skiing alone off-piste or flying to an offshore rig to spend a month doing geophysical data acquisition, staying in a safe place has never interested me. I have been the Science Officer on an oceanographic ship, laid sea bottom seismic cables and worked cattle on horseback in Brazil. My education has enabled this lifestyle. An Electrical Engineering degree followed by a Masters in Geophysics opened the doors to jobs that required a local presence. It took me out there.

Science fiction and sailing ship adventures have always been an important part of my life since a child. Like most kids, I have dreamed of being a spacer, going to faraway places, having adventure and romance. Since so few actually get to go out even in humanity's current limited way, I have shaped my life to get out into our world. I always like to think that locked up in an instrumentation shed in the middle of nowhere is a little like being in space.

Roswell Boneyard

I live with my wife of decades. We currently split our time between Texas and SW Brazil. But who knows what tomorrow will bring?

Printed in Great Britain
by Amazon